THE POWER OF ONE

By

W. Foster Welborn

If you would like to contact me:

My Website is: **www.wfosterwelborn.com**
for information, Email and feedback on this
book.

My Mailing Address is:

> PO Box 745865
> Arvada, CO 80006-5865

This book is available at:

https://www.createspace.com/4009384

or Amazon.com and also from the
Amazon.com Kindle Store under my author
name or book title.

To My Wife, Mary Lou,

Who loves my stories,

Encourages and puts up with me.

My Other Books on Kindle:

The Power of Two (Sequel to this book)

Smoking Earth River

Dah-A-Sah

Autumn Leaves

THE POWER OF ONE, BOOK 1:

Table of Contents

PREFACE

David could not explain his power any more than I can. Any attempt on his part would be as feeble as mine trying to explain the infinite, intangible something which lies deep inside each of us upon this majestic planet we call Earth.

There is a special something, unseen by the eyes, untouched by hands, and unheard with our ears, yet always lurking just on the horizons of our consciousness.

It is a power possessed to some degree by each of us and brought forth by our depth of awareness. We are bound only by our ability to think, our daring to utilize our imagination, and our willingness to achieve.

Plenty of books have been written on various subjects such as energy fields, time dimensions, telepathy, UFO's, telekinesis, stars, planets and so forth—enough to fill many libraries.

Many books attempt to explain, reason, verify, dispute, analyze, or discuss these subjects toward some conclusion. None of them are adequate to satisfactorily explain the ether of the human spirit.

Then too, there are those pesky unexplained occurrences in places such as Lourdes—strange happenings such as alien space craft, UFO's, Area #51, wondrous miracle cures and healings. There is any number of unusual events such as déjà vu— occurrences which many of us have read about or maybe even experienced in one form or another.

Most of our books cannot adequately explain the miracle of birth, why or how we age and die, or how we are able to continue breathing even as we sleep. Of course, we are all taught that our brain regulates our breathing, but another question makes itself manifest. How is our brain programmed to do this? It had to be programmed before we drew our first breath. So, how does it occur, or should I ask who programmed our brain?

Remember, no one knows for certain. Much of our knowledge is simply theory—that is to say…some person's opinion. In many cases, these theories are accepted simply because the various subject matters cannot be explained satisfactorily any other way.

Put another way, we simply do not possess the necessary knowledge or even an adequate vocabulary to conduct an explanation into words of some of these wondrous events and occurrences.

We are still struggling to explain the building of the Egyptian pyramids, Machu Picchu, and Mesoamerican pyramids. How were they built and by whom?

Think about it for a moment. We cannot explain Stonehenge, Atlantis, or even the Bermuda Triangle! There are numerous places, events and concepts which tantalize our imagination and tease our intelligence.

Now along comes David Michaels. Did he really possess power to accomplish all the things written about him? Can we prove or disprove it, or maybe in some way measure or test his power?

Probably what most of us would like to do is place these strange occurrences and concepts in a little box all tied up neatly with a pretty ribbon, placed on a shelf and tucked away into the dust bins of our minds.

In this manner, we are able to cope on our very own chosen level of understanding. We then have absolute control of our comfort zone.

Still, in quiet moments, when we stop or shut down the motor and make contact with that secret place deep within us, the unanswerable questions once more begin to tease and taunt us.

This is the story of David Michaels, who could not explain his gift either. We will let you be the judge and draw your own conclusions.

W. Foster Welborn

CHAPTER 1

David Michaels entered this world at two o'clock in the morning on the seventh day of March in the year of 1939. He took his first breath of Texas air in the town of Corpus Christi and tipped the scales at exactly seven pounds.

His mother, Julie, and father, Bob, had awaited and anticipated his arrival with great expectation and joy.

Bob was a very good carpenter who worked building single family homes when he was not going a few rounds with the bottle. He was basically a decent man with one big weakness. He could not leave the booze alone. When he got drunk, he would become mean and ugly.

Julie Michaels had worked hard to put herself through college. Finally, the long-awaited day arrived when she officially became a registered nurse. It was one of the happiest days of her life.

After her graduation, Bob had crawled into the bottle and become completely drunk. He had made some nasty remarks to Julie, partly out of jealousy. One thing led to another. In a drunken stupor, he struck her, knocking her to the floor. Not only was the blow painful, but it scared her even more. She did not know if he would hurt the child, but she sure did not plan to stick around and find out.

With money she had saved, Julie packed two suitcases and left Corpus Christi with little David while Bob was passed out drunk on the floor. She did not even leave a note!

Julie and David, traveling by bus, arrived one day and a half later in Aurora, Colorado. After a few days in an inexpensive motel, she landed a job at Fitzsimons Army Hospital. Later, she found a small apartment. She and little David, who was three years' old, began a new life. Getting started had been hard, but Julie was determined. Little by little, she made headway. Julie was very careful with her earnings and maintained an austere budget. While she and David did not live a life of luxury, they did quite well. Julie continued her nursing career at Fitzsimons, earning distinction as an outstanding nurse, well respected by her peers.

Every morning, she made breakfast for the two of them, and then made each of them a lunch in neat brown paper bags.

After school, while most young people his age were out tossing a baseball or football around, enjoying their childhood, David would come home from school and let himself in with his own key. Then he would attempt to cook something hot for their supper. Because of the tight budget, David could not try anything really fancy. Still, he became a decent cook for his age. His favorite dishes were macaroni and cheese alongside meatloaf. He was also very handy when it came to cleaning and dusting. In these ways, he helped his Mom as much as he could. David could see how tired she was when she came home in the evening. His reward was the grateful look of appreciation in her eyes. She would always say something like, "I don't know what I'd do without you, Davey boy," or "I love you, Davey. You are so helpful."

David stood five feet ten inches tall and weighed one hundred and sixty pounds. He was on the lanky side with brown hair, long sideburns, with brown eyebrows arched over clear blue eyes. His eyes were separated by a small nose which was sprinkled with freckles. A shock of brown hair arched up and came down about a half inch over his right eye, giving David's face a mischievous quality.

One day, as David was walking home from school, he was struck by a speeding car when he was crossing a street. Bystanders told the Police that the driver was operating the vehicle in an erratic, reckless manner, suggesting the driver was under the influence of alcohol.

All David remembered was the instant shock and pain from impact before he lost complete consciousness. Everything faded into darkness even as an ambulance whisked him to the Emergency Room at University of Colorado Hospital.

In the Emergency Room, he was treated for contusions and abrasions to his head, fractured ribs and compound fractures to both legs. Coupled with all these problems, David had lapsed into a coma. He lay motionless on the hospital bed, except for his breathing. Both legs were in casts and elevated in traction. His rib cage was taped up tightly due to fractures.

Nurse Johnson placed a needle into David's left arm and taped it securely. She attached an IV drip bag on a stand by the bed and started the drip so the young patient could be fed intravenously. She checked his pulse and then made notes on his medical chart at the end of the bed.

"Poor thing," she thought as she gazed into his face. "He looks so young and frail!"

She knew how much effort had gone into the x-rays, casts, consultations and diagnoses by the doctors.

"David Michaels, you are so lucky to be alive!" she whispered.

David was unaware of any of this due to the coma.

CHAPTER 2

While David did not know where he was, he realized he was moving very fast. He could see stars very close to him as he traveled. He could see the Earth behind him, big and majestic, but growing smaller and smaller as stars and meteors grew bigger and closer.

His velocity was so fast that colors seemed to dance and blur together before his eyes. Strangely, he felt very warm. When he glanced behind him, he could see a very thin, almost transparent ribbon stretching back into infinity. It seemed to be attached to his back.

David was too young and inexperienced to even ponder what might be happening to him. In all of his acquired but limited knowledge, he knew nothing concerning out-of-body experiences.

David closed his eyes, hoping that, when he opened them again, he would snap out of this impossible dream. In a short while, he opened his eyes.

"I'm not dreaming. This is real!" he muttered to himself.

He could see before him a silver-blue planet glowing softly in the distance. As he approached nearer the surface, different shapes and features began to appear. He could make out a gleaming city, but it was unlike anything he had ever seen. There before him were spheres atop lofty spires, bathed in a subdued slate-blue light. Strange stream-lined conveyances moved about the city, almost ghost-like. There were no wailing sirens or blinking red lights. Most noticeably, there was none of the noise associated with an Earth city as he knew it.

David closed his eyes again, determined to awaken from this amazingly real dream. While his eyes were closed, he felt his body come to a complete stop. David just knew the dream would be over when he opened his eyes.

He thought, "After all, I've not really been moving in the first place—especially through space! I've just been hallucinating and must be terribly confused."

Nevertheless, when his body stopped moving, it had come to rest on a couch.

When he opened his eyes, the first thing he noticed was the transparent thread of ribbon pooled up next to the couch. This couch had a beige-colored satin-like fabric. Overhead, there were soft indirect lights shining from recessed gray-colored panels.

David looked at his body, not knowing if he should be afraid or not. He still felt that all of this must simply be a dream.

He could see the room was an off-white color. It contained glass panels with the appearance of mirrors going completely around the room.

There was an arched doorway to the room, but with no door attached. The floor had a highly-polished sheen and looked like light colored grey marble.

Movement in the doorway caused David to blink in a mixture of fear and surprise as a tall lady entered the room. For a moment, his breath caught in his throat as she approached him.

He thought, "I've never seen a more radiant-looking lady in all my life!"

There was an aura of white dazzling light about her as she moved forward. She wore a flowing white gown gathered at the waist with an intricately woven, golden girdle. As she moved, David could see finely worked golden sandals on her dainty feet. Her long golden hair was held at the forehead by a small golden tiara. She looked a lot like the women of Planet Earth, except her complexion was flawless, with a translucent quality and was much more radiant.

She stopped a few feet from him. For some unknown reason, David's fear left him as he looked into the eyes of this lovely being.

She smiled.

Suddenly, David began experiencing thoughts which he knew were not his own.

"Welcome to our Planet, Gorbandihar! My name is Miranda. What is yours?"

David gasped in surprise as he thought, "Did this lady or being just speak to me? Her lips did not move. I did not hear any sounds. Yet I feel certain she just spoke to me! I've read several science fiction books and seen movies about spaceships and spacemen. I often wondered how a person would go about speaking to an alien."

Once again, his thoughts were interrupted.

"In fact, I am not an alien. Since you are on our planet, you are the alien. Please tell me your name."

David was speechless.

"Man," he thought, "this is so cool!" as he looked at her.

Touching himself on the chest with his thumb, David thought as he mouthed the words, "My name is David Michaels, and I came here from Planet Earth."

"Very good," she replied, speaking the words out loud this time. "I should speak the words in your language instead of thinking them so you won't be frightened. What does cool mean?"

David managed a little laugh. Now he was beginning to relax and enjoy the situation.

"Oh, we just call it a figure of speech on Earth. It means very good in slang," he replied.

"What is slang?" she asked. "Is it an Earth language?"

David hesitated before answering.

"This is going to be difficult to explain because, in truth, I don't always understand all the slang myself. No," he replied, "it's not really a language. It's just a silly, short form of speaking that the young people on my planet use."

David looked at the pretty lady and finally asked the question he was dying to ask: "How did I get here?"

Miranda smiled as she spoke, "You were summoned."

"By who?" asked David in amazement.

"Why, by He Who Summons," she replied, still smiling.

"But I don't understand why," stammered David.

"Don't worry," she smiled as she answered. "No one knows why He does what He does. He just does, that's all. Now I've been selected by He Who Summons to act as your tutor, guide and guardian while you are on our planet."

Gathering his courage, David asked, "Are you human beings, like us?"

Miranda smiled her marvelous smile.

"No, we are beings that are more like spirit than human in form," she answered.

"Are there teenagers like me on your planet?" quizzed David.

"I'm not sure," stated Miranda. "What is a teenager?"

David explained about age and the difference in being either young or old.

"Yes, we do have younger and older beings here, but we don't age like human beings do," responded Miranda, again with a smile.

David returned her smile and tentatively ventured one more question. He explained about asking Earth women their age and then asked sheepishly if he could ask her age.

Miranda's smile broadened as she answered with no hesitation, "I'm one hundred fifty years old as you measure time on your planet."

David gulped in astonishment, "You don't look a day over twenty-five in my estimation!"

This brought an even broader smile from Miranda.

"Enough questions! We must begin!" she said.

Miranda reached out her hand toward David's head. Immediately, there appeared a dome of gold light in the shape of a half crescent which remained there. Next she pointed her hand towards the glass panels, which began displaying pictures in vivid colors of changing scenes and pictures of Earth.

David watched the changing panels with fascination.

He wondered, "My Mom recently purchased a small television, but the pictures are all black and white. How could the beings on this planet possibly have pictures of Earth—in color?"

Miranda intercepted his thoughts and spoke, "What you see here is but a very small feat of technology for us. These changing pictures will serve as teaching guides for you.

You must concentrate! There is a tremendous amount of information for you to absorb, with limited time available."

Unknown to David, the soft golden glowing device above his head would act as a booster to increase his mental capacity, using brain cell manipulation. This would enable him to absorb and retain huge volumes of information.

David felt a sense of curiosity, coupled with urgency, as he stepped toward Miranda. Inherently, he knew that the process he was about to undertake would entail a journey in learning, covering areas so diverse and challenging that it would turn most of Earth's scholars green with envy.

David was taught not only the secrets but the mysteries of Life. The instruction included solutions for various problems in health and healing. Not only was this information absorbed, but it was imprinted in such a manner that David would not forget it.

"Why was I chosen?" he thought.

It was a question he could not answer, nor did he care. He was here and eager to learn everything Miranda wished to teach him.

When David considered the situation, he realized, "This is the utmost in cool!"

.

CHAPTER 3

Julie Michaels was busy at her work station when the phone call came from University of Colorado Hospital about David. She almost dropped the receiver in shock. Her heart was beating rapidly as she listened to an explanation from a nurse in the Emergency Room. Tears formed in her eyes as she listened.

One of her co-workers noticed the tears in her eyes and said, "What is wrong?"

"My son has been in an automobile accident," Julie stammered haltingly. "He is in the Emergency Room at the University of Colorado Hospital! They need my signature on some forms," she said, wringing her hands nervously.

Her co-worker wrapped her arm around Julie's shoulder.

"It's going to be all right. We'll get the floor supervisor's OK and get you down there," she stated.

Julie's fellow workers and supervisor were very understanding and helpful. Not ten minutes had elapsed before she was in a fellow worker's car being driven to that Hospital.

Julie dabbed at the stream of tears flowing freely, while her mind went back over hers and David's life together.

"It's been a life of hard work and struggle. Yet, there have been many bright moments and shared laughter. My memories of his quick smile and eager willingness to help just keep my tears flowing!"

"I've seen many children with different sicknesses, diseases, broken bones, and any number of ailments, but I've always coped because I'm a professional and go about my duties accordingly. But this is different. This is my son, and my love and hopes for him break down any professional attitude on my part. I live and work for David."

As the car sped toward the Hospital, she thought, "The idea of David being hurt is almost unbearable! The thought of losing him is unthinkable!"

Her co-worker dropped Julie off in front of the Emergency Room and drove out of the entrance to find a parking space.

With dread and a heavy heart, Julie entered the Emergency Room. She realized that she had not even taken the time to change out of her uniform as she approached the nurse at the desk.

"May I help you?" asked the nurse, whose name plate bore the name Johnson.

"Yes, my name is Julie Michaels. My son, David, was brought in here for treatment," she answered.

"Oh, yes," replied Nurse Johnson. "Follow me, please."

She then led the way to a curtained-off area of the Emergency Room. She pulled aside the sliding curtain and Julie, with bated breath, entered.

Julie's heart was in her throat as she gazed at her son.

"He looks so pale!" she thought as she wiped tears from her eyes.

She could see that David was hooked up to a heart monitor machine, and he lay there completely motionless, except for his breathing. His legs were in casts and suspended in slings, and his rib cage was wrapped tightly with tape.

Nurse Johnson then explained the extent of David's injuries as she consulted his medical charts. Julie listened to her in silent anguish.

"We need your signature on some forms, as you well know," Nurse Johnson continued with a smile. "We've already taken x-rays, and we've set the bones in both legs and obviously put casts on them."

Julie nodded and asked, "Is there anything else I can do?"

"No, there's nothing I can think of to do except to wait," replied Nurse Johnson. "That is the hardest part."

Julie signed the consent forms as well as all the insurance forms.

She thought, "Now I understand what other parents go through during traumatic times when their loved ones are admitted to the hospital for treatment. I vow to be more compassionate and understanding when dealing with the parents of patients in the future!"

After completing the paperwork, Julie sat on a chair next to David's bed. There was nothing to do now but wait and pray.

CHAPTER 4

Once Miranda was completely satisfied that David's learning process had been completed successfully, she removed the golden crescent from above his head.

David did not notice any difference in the way he felt.

Miranda gave a smile of approval.

"Tell no one anything concerning the things you've seen and learned here, David. Your people are not ready to accept what you know. In your slang words, it would not be cool!" She laughed. "Besides, they would never believe you could travel through space without a pressurized spaceship and oxygen anyway."

Because of her infectious laugh, David could not suppress a grin and said, "The newspaper reporters would hound me to death if they caught wind of this information."

She nodded her head in agreement.

"It's time you returned to your own people and planet, but just remember, while there is much good you can do with your new knowledge and power, you must exercise

24

caution. It's better to do your good works in secret, away from prying eyes. Besides, it's very doubtful if anyone would believe you could possess such power. More than likely, they would accuse you of working magic, or…worse yet…witch craft. Because of their religious teaching and upbringing, they, in turn, would cause you much grief."

David listened to her words intently, knowing in his heart that this lovely creature spoke the truth.

"Two last things to remember," she continued. "We've imprinted your mind in such a manner that we can track you on our instruments, which have been programmed to receive your thought patterns. Our instruments will also inform us when you harness healing energy and utilize it to heal. You will not feel any different nor will you experience any discomfort. In this way, we can check on your progress and know your location."

"The second and last point is simply that, for whatever reason, you have been chosen above all others and given this gift freely. Use it wisely. Above all else, accept no reward or payment for your healing and good works. He Who Summons absolutely insists on this last point and asked me to stress it most strongly. This I have done."

"Now, David Michaels, my work is complete. There is nothing left except to wish you good luck and a safe journey home."

David smiled and thanked her as she turned and moved out of the room.

He thought, "I'm always amazed because she seems to float over the floor rather than walk on it! I feel a lonely, cold emptiness in the pit of my stomach. I miss her wonderful smile and warm radiance already!"

CHAPTER 5

Once more David felt himself moving through space away from the silver-blue planet he now knew as Gorbandihar.

He thought, "I have no concept of speed or time as I gaze at the celestial beauty of space around me! It's mind boggling, but I'm unafraid because I now possess an understanding of what is taking place. There's no heat, cold or even wind whistling in my ears as one would experience while riding in a car with the windows down. I realize why I require no oxygen, pressurized spaceship or suit to move through this space. As a matter of fact, atomic radiation and magnetic pull have no effect on my spirit form as it would a flesh-and-blood human body!"

David reveled in the beauty of space as he moved ever closer toward the majestic blue and white planet he knew as home.

He thought, "I will never again take life for granted!"

As he traveled, David recalled the teaching room where he was surrounded by scenes and machines.

He thought, "The golden crescent above my head made everything easy to understand. Subject matter that would have confused doctors, lawyers, mathematicians, scientists, clergy and anyone else exposed to it was made simple and crystal clear to me. My time of receiving information moved with such startling speed. I wonder if it is not just a blurred dream instead of reality. When I'm safely back on Earth, maybe my dream will come to an end."

"I feel extreme sadness about leaving the Planet Gorbandihar behind because all of the inhabitants I met were so friendly and happy. They were in many respects just like humans in appearance, but there the similarity ended. The first thing I noticed was their cooperation with one another. I did not see any of them express anger towards anyone, and one of them informed me that war was unknown to the inhabitants of Gorbandihar. They never experience disease or any kind of sickness, nor do they eat food like Earthlings."

"The conveyances used to move these beings around their city are marvelous to behold. They are powered by particle thrusters. They are very fast, but at the same time, very quiet. When I rode in one, I realized just how far advanced the inhabitants of Gorbandihar are over humans. They are Light

Years ahead of us! Compared to them, we are still babes in the woods!"

Approaching ever closer to Earth, David could begin to distinguish some of the landmarks close to his home. The front range of the Rocky Mountains began looming on the horizon. His forward momentum began slowing drastically. Suddenly, a hospital appeared before him as he approached closer.

David closed his eyes and felt his body slow ever so gently and come to a stop.

When he opened his eyes, the first thing he noticed was that both of his legs were in casts and elevated up above his head with white slings! His rib cage was wrapped tightly with tape, and his left arm hurt badly!

"So it was only a dream after all," he thought.

He realized that he was in a hospital when another fact hit him full force.

"Oh, my gosh! The pain! My legs and ribs hurt like the dickens!"

There was a needle taped to his left arm which had a clear tube attached to a plastic bottle on a stand above him. This accounted for the pain he felt in his arm. He looked around the room with a puzzled expression on his young face.

He experienced a panic rising in the pit of his stomach.

He wondered, "What happened? Where exactly am I and why?"

CHAPTER 6

Nurse Betty Lewis was checking the medical chart at the foot of his bed when she noticed David's eyelids fluttered and his head moved.

Immediately, she left the room and trotted towards the Nurse's Station.

"Doctor Hollis," she called, her voice charged with excitement. "He's regained consciousness."

Doctor Hollis looked at her like she had just stepped off another planet until what she had said registered in his brain. Instantly, his face lit in recognition as he trotted down the hallway and disappeared into David's room.

Quickly, he moved over beside David's bed, and as he did so, he thought, "Sure enough, my young patient is lying quietly, gazing around the room. For someone coming out of a coma, his blue eyes are clear and his face has a puzzled expression. I wonder what he is thinking?"

Doctor Hollis lifted David's right wrist and checked his pulse while intently looking at his watch.

"Welcome back to the land of the living, young man," he said. "We were beginning to worry about you."

He placed his stethoscope on David's chest and listened closely. After a few moments, he stepped back while looking at the youngster's face.

"All of your vital signs are elevated because of your pain. How do you feel, David?" he asked.

"I feel pain in my legs and ribs, and my left arm hurts a lot. Why are my legs in casts and elevated in slings, and why is my rib cage wrapped with tape, Doctor?" David asked. "Where am I anyway?" he added before Doctor Hollis could speak.

Doctor Hollis smiled and answered, "You don't remember the accident, do you? You were struck by a car while crossing a street. An ambulance brought you here to the University of Colorado Hospital. For the last fourteen days, you've been in a coma."

David's face mirrored his surprise as he listened to the Doctor's explanation.

"You say I've been here for fourteen whole days? That is unbelievable!" he said.

"Yep," replied Doctor Hollis, "and your Mom has been here every night, sitting up with you."

David looked at the needle in his left arm, held securely in place with adhesive tape. The skin around the needle was red and inflamed. A dull throbbing pain moved up his arm.

David thought, "How could I have been gone for fourteen days and nights? The time duration seemed like only a few short hours. Maybe I just dreamed the whole thing up after all!"

Doctor Hollis watched David's eyes move from the needle in his arm over to make eye contact with him.

"That thing hurts, Doctor," David said matter-of-factly. "When can you take it out?"

Doctor Hollis responded, "When that IV is finished—which will occur shortly— we'll have the needle removed, but you have to promise me you will eat. How about it, are you hungry?"

"You bet!" David said, grinning widely. "Bet you a plugged nickel I could eat at least four hamburgers with fries and a big chocolate malt right now…that is, if I could get them."

Doctor Hollis nodded in satisfaction because a good appetite bode well for his patient.

"I think you are on the road to recovery. I will call your Mom and give her the good news!" he told David. "I've got to finish my rounds and check on my other patients. I will leave instructions to have the needle removed when that drip is finished. I'm sorry we can't promise you hamburgers and fries, but I will have them bring you some dinner."

David nodded in response as he watched the Doctor leave his room. He attempted to move his legs a little to get more comfortable and was rewarded with a sharp pain in both legs for his effort. He stole a quick glance towards the door to ensure no one was near.

Satisfied that he was alone, David figured, "Now is as good a time as any to find out if I've only been dreaming or not, or if I do, in truth, have any real power."

Without further hesitation, he began moving his hands over his injured ribs. At once, he could feel the warmth radiating through the skin and into the bones. Strangely, almost as if by divine guidance, David applied healing knowledge through the radiating heat emanating from his hands. He began to experience his ribs fusing and returning to normal.

"Wow! The pain in my ribs has completely disappeared!" he thought ecstatically.

David experienced both shock and elation at the same time.

"It wasn't a dream after all! I do have healing power! I did make the trip to Gorbandihar!" he thought.

Nervously, he again glanced towards the door to assure himself that he was alone and unobserved. Next he raised himself up enough to position his hands over the breaks in his legs. This position was painfully awkward, and sweat popped out on his face and forehead. Still, he continued to administer the healing waves of heat through his hands.

Once more, he could feel the glowing penetration of heat. As the breaks began to fuse, his waves of pain eased off and began to subside. David grunted in satisfaction as the pain diminished and faded away. He fell back on the bed and mopped sweat from his face with his right hand.

David did not realize that, as the pain disappeared, his vital signs became almost normal.

"There," he whispered. "I'm almost finished. All the pain is gone, except for the throbbing pain in my arm."

"Oh, man," he thought. "I do have power and knowledge! Miranda was real and so was the miraculous gift I've been given!"

David felt like shouting. He wanted to celebrate, call a nurse and show her what he could do. In that same moment, he realized that he could undertake none of those actions.

"In fact, I cannot tell a single soul!" he thought. "Wasn't I severely warned about this by Miranda? Oh, but man, it is ever so cool! No one on Earth has this knowledge and power. It was given to me!"

A giddy feeling came over him.

"Not only can I not tell another soul—I cannot even tell my Mom!"

CHAPTER 7

Julie Michaels picked up the receiver and said, "Hello."

It was early afternoon and she was at work when Doctor Hollis called her. Her heart was beating like a trip hammer as she tried to prepare herself for the worst.

"Hello, Mrs. Michaels. I have some very good news for you. David has recovered consciousness a short while ago. He's talking and says he's really hungry!" He chuckled and continued, "As you know, this is a wonderful sign!"

Julie listened quietly, tears of relief streaming down her face. The relief flooded through every nerve and fiber in her body. Her knees felt weak as she struggled to gain control of her emotions. She felt like shouting.

"Mrs. Michaels, are you there? Can you hear me?" asked Doctor Hollis.

The words just tumbled out of her now: "Yes, Doctor, I can hear you just fine. It's just that I've been so worried and under such a strain. I was so afraid of what I might hear, and now I'm so relieved! It'll take a moment for me to collect myself. I'm sorry," she spoke softly through tears of joy.

Doctor Hollis heard the emotion in her voice.

"David is going to be just fine, Mrs. Michaels. He says he can eat four hamburgers with fries and a big chocolate malt," and then he laughed again.

A small laugh escaped Julie's lips as she said, "Chocolate malts are his favorite."

Doctor Hollis had to go but he said lightly, "I know he'll be looking forward to seeing you. Will you be coming to visit later this evening or tonight?"

"Yes," replied Julie. "I'll be there as soon as I get off work."

"That's great, Mrs. Michaels. I'll tell him you're coming in a little while. I'll talk more with you later. Just wanted you to know he's doing really well so you wouldn't worry, OK?" Dr. Hollis said gently.

"Thank you, Doctor. I do sincerely appreciate your call," she said as she hung up the phone.

Then she went to the Ladies Room and had a good cry. All the pain, worry, tension and pent-up emotions came pouring out with her tears. When she dried her eyes and looked into the mirror, she realized she was a disheveled mess. After washing her face, she patted her hair back into place, applied some touch up on her makeup and went back to work.

Her heart was light now as she thought, "David's going to be all right! I recall the horror of the phone call, informing me of the accident. I remember the fear and emotions as I waited in the Visitors' Lounge, coupled with the long visits, the waiting, praying and hoping for David to regain consciousness. I vividly recall the quiet moments in my room on my knees in prayer, and now," she smiled radiantly, "I know that God does indeed answer prayers!"

She contemplated, "Being a single parent is not easy. There never seems to be enough time in the day. There is always work to do and bills to pay. Like all parents, I want to do things with David. I try very hard to spend time with him on weekends. Usually during work days, I'm very tired when I arrive home from being on my feet all day. David, bless his heart, not only has his homework completed but also does his very best to prepare something hot for us to eat. He's such a wonderful boy! He deserves the very best I can give him. My heartfelt wish is that I can have more time to spend with him!"

She glanced at the clock and began making preparations for shift change at her Nurse's Station. When she had filled out her timecard and said her daily farewells, she stopped in the Ladies Room to freshen her makeup.

Once outside the hospital, she caught a bus towards downtown and got off a few blocks away from University of Colorado Hospital. She stopped at a restaurant a couple of blocks away from the hospital and ordered hamburgers, fries, and two chocolate malts to go. The smell of the burgers and fries made her stomach rumble. Julie realized she was hungry.

"Great!" she thought. "But tonight, I will be able to eat a meal with my son!"

That thought filled her with joy.

Once inside the hospital, her shoes beat a rhythmic tattoo on the polished hallway as she moved towards the elevators. When she reached the right floor, she walked down the hallway to the Nurse's Station. Nurse Lewis, upon noticing her, beamed a big friendly smile at her as she came around the counter and linked her arm through Julie's. Together they walked through the doorway to David's room.

Nurse Lewis stopped and stood back as Julie rushed to the bedside and bent over, smothering David's face with kisses.

"Aw, come on, Mom," David sputtered, giving a little laugh.

Julie's heart leapt for joy to see how embarrassed he was and hear his so typical remark. These removed the last shadows of doubt from her mind.

She thought, "My son is indeed OK!"

Out loud, she said, "Look what I've brought," as she beamed, holding the bag out towards him.

His nose had already told him what the contents were as she began setting the goodies out on the rollaway table.

"Did you bring enough for both of us, Mom?" asked David grinning.

"You bet your bottom dollar, Davey boy," she replied softly.

41

Nurse Lewis quietly backed out of the room to enable mother and son privacy and to enjoy their little meal and each other in peace. It was moments like this which made Nurse Lewis love her profession.

Julie sat on the opposite side of the bed from David's left arm so as not to cause him any pain. She opened catsup and placed it on a paper saucer for dipping the French fries. She also opened salt and pepper packets for their hamburgers and fries.

She looked at her son's face as a shadowy grimace of pain caused his face to wrinkle and corners of his lips turn down.

"What's the matter, Son? Are you in a lot of pain?" she asked, looking at him concerned.

"Actually, Mom, this needle hurts more than anything," he said, smiling weakly.

Both of them began eating and enjoying the food.

He smiled at his Mom, saying, "It's very good, Mom, thanks."

She returned his smile as she said, "It wasn't any trouble at all. I know how much you like them."

David thought, "It's so great, having Mom here, but secretly, I wish she wasn't here so I could relieve the pain in my arm."

Immediately, he felt very guilty for having such a thought.

David endured the pain and put on as brave a face as he could while he and his Mom talked.

Shortly, Julie stood up and cleared away the paper, empty condiment packets and malt cups. She smiled at David, bent over and kissed him on the cheek.

"You know, I've got to get home, as bad as I hate to leave you. There are little chores I have to take care of before I can go to bed," she said.

"What kind of chores have you got to do, Mom?" asked David curiously.

"For one thing, I have to iron a uniform for tomorrow," she answered.

"Oh, I had forgotten," murmured David.

She took his right hand and held it next to her cheek.

"I'm so glad you're going to be all right. I was so scared and worried about you!" she said as tears filled her eyes. "I couldn't stand the thought of losing you, Davey. I just don't know what I'd have done without you!"

"It's going to be OK, Mom. I'm here and I'm not going anywhere," he stammered.

Julie smiled and dried her eyes.

"I'll come back tomorrow night and see you. Do you want me to bring you anything special?" she asked.

David was silent because he knew how tight their money situation was, so he replied, "No, Mom. I don't need anything at all. They'll take good care of me here, so you don't need to worry about anything, OK?"

Julie smiled and said, "OK, buddy. I'll see you tomorrow night."

As she moved towards the doorway, she turned towards him and blew him a kiss with her hand.

She stopped by the Nurse's Station to thank Nurse Lewis for caring for David and then went on to the elevators. She knew she needed to get home and get some rest. The ordeal of the last few weeks, the worry over David's coma and injuries, and now the joy at seeing him simply overwhelmed her. Tears slipped freely down her face as she made her way home.

She just kept thinking, "He's going to be OK!"

Relief flooded her being.

"Maybe tonight I will be able to sleep," she thought, as a yawn escaped her.

CHAPTER 8

David reached to push the call button for the nurse and waited patiently. After a few minutes, the same pretty blonde nurse entered the room wearing a friendly smile.

He returned her smile while pointing towards the empty IV bag and spoke, "Can you please remove the needle now? It hurts like the dickens."

"You betcha!" she replied as she deftly but gently began removing the tape securing the needle in place.

David could see that the flesh surrounding the needle was red and angry looking.

"My name is Nurse Betty Lewis," she told him as she tossed the tape into a trash container.

Carefully, she removed the needle and swabbed the area with an alcohol-saturated cotton swab.

"The redness will go away in a day or so," she said.

David exhaled a large sigh of relief as he rubbed his arm. Unconsciously, he applied heat through his hand while willing the pain to go away. He was using his healing techniques as a reflex gesture to ease the pain. As he did so, he looked at his arm.

"Whoa!" he thought excitedly. "Not only did the pain vanish immediately, but so did the puncture wound and the angry red skin surrounding the needle hole! Awesome!"

However, almost immediately, David realized he had made a mistake as he pulled the bedspread up over his arm, hoping Nurse Lewis had not seen what just happened.

"Dog gone it!" he thought. "After all my instruction and training, I am already being careless! What in the world was I thinking anyway? I can see that learning the extent of my power and how and when to apply it is going to take some time and practice. I am going to have to use more caution! Miranda was right! I will have to do my acts of healing in secret or else I'll get myself into big trouble!"

Unknown to David, Nurse Lewis had, indeed, seen out of the corner of her eyes that the needle puncture mark and angry red skin had disappeared from his arm while he was rubbing it. She was filled with astonishment, but she composed her face into a straight-forward look of innocence.

"I do not understand how such a thing could happen," she told herself, "but I do know what I just witnessed with my own eyes!"

She turned to go out of the door when an idea occurred to her.

Acting on a sudden impulse, she turned toward David and asked, "How do your legs feel? Can you wiggle your toes a little?"

David smiled and, without thinking, wiggled his toes on both feet, and for good measure, he rotated his feet in small half circles.

Nurse Lewis observed his face closely for any sign of pain. She was surprised and baffled too!

She thought, "How could he possibly make such movements with compound fractures in both legs? Yet his face is serene and displaying no visible signs of pain whatever!"

Another idea came to her, so she said, "David, I need to take your vital signs one more time, OK?"

Again, she found a surprise.

"Why, all his vital signs are now normal. How can this be?" she wondered.

Nurse Lewis maintained a poker face as she went towards the door.

"I'll have your dinner brought in if you're still hungry," she said to David.

"I think I'll pass on dinner," David replied with a smile. "The hamburgers, fries, and malt filled me up pretty good. Thanks, anyway."

"OK," she smiled and said, "I'll check on you later."

He watched her go, unaware that she knew what had just happened.

"She's really cool," he thought, "and pretty too."

When Nurse Lewis got to the Nurse's Station, she first lifted the phone and dialed the hospital kitchen.

When the kitchen staff answered, she said, "Please place David Michaels in Room 110 on the regular feeding schedule, starting tomorrow morning."

She was still wondering about what she had just seen, perplexed by the whole scene as she replayed it in her mind.

She thought, "I need to discuss this with Dr. Hollis!"

She then set about locating him and found out that he was taking a break in the staff lounge. Nurse Lewis entered the lounge area just as Doctor Hollis was throwing his empty coffee cup into a trash container prior to leaving.

"Doctor Hollis, can I speak to you for a moment?" she asked.

"Sure, Nurse Lewis, what's going on?" he said as he sat down on the arm of a sofa and looked at her expectantly.

"It's about our young patient in Room 110, Doctor," she said.

"So, what about David Michaels?" asked Doctor Hollis. "When I checked him, he was doing really well. He has a good appetite.

I'd say he'll be out of the woods as soon as his legs and ribs mend."

"That's what I want to talk to you about, Doctor," replied Nurse Lewis hesitantly. "I think he might be doing too well! Would you believe that his vital signs are all normal now?"

"What in heaven's name are you saying, Nurse Lewis?" he asked—while his face wore a puzzled expression.

Nurse Lewis took a deep breath, carefully looked around to be certain no one could eavesdrop on their conversation, and launched into a brief but thoroughly accurate description of what she had observed.

Doctor Hollis listened to Nurse Lewis' explanation, his face changing from puzzlement to one of disbelief.

"You are surely kidding me! That's impossible!" he stated as he exhaled with a snort.

"All I know, Doctor, is that I've never seen anything like it during my entire career, but I know what I saw with these baby blues. Besides, I just thought you would want to know," she said simply.

Doctor Hollis looked into Nurse Lewis' face for a long moment. He did not doubt her sincerity or truthfulness for a moment. In fact, he trusted her judgment completely. She was one of the most professional nurses he had ever worked with during his career.

"For the time being, Nurse Lewis, let's just keep this between you and me. I'll look in on him again as soon as I finish my rounds," he said.

She replied, "Great, Doctor, but please do me a small favor. When you've seen him, how about stopping by the Nurse's Station and let me know what you think about his condition."

"Yes, Ma'am, Nurse Lewis!" he said as he smiled and gave her a mock salute as he turned and walked out of the lounge.

Nurse Lewis smiled too as she strolled back to the Nurse's Station.

"Doctor Hollis is a very handsome man, and he just happens to be single, just like me," she thought.

Continuing to ponder on David, she thought, "I know that my eyes did not play tricks on me. Maybe I just witnessed a real miracle! Does young David possess some supernatural power? I cannot explain the incident, but I know something strange certainly took place!"

She busied herself with medication schedules and medical charts. As always, there was no end to the paperwork required during her daily routine. Staying busy helped to keep her mind occupied, and the hours seemed to evaporate. She was still busy with paperwork when Doctor Hollis' voice interrupted her concentration.

"Yes, Ma'am, Nurse Lewis, I do see what you mean," he said nonchalantly, giving her another playful salute. "As soon as you can, I want you to get an x-ray technician up here with a mobile x-ray machine. I want pictures of his ribs and both legs stat!"

He extended a sheet of paper to her.

"Here's a note for the technician with my instructions," he said.

Now he leaned over the counter and whispered softly to her, "It's really amazing! There's no way he should have that much range of motion without experiencing extreme pain during movement! Maybe the x-rays will show us what his status really is."

Nurse Lewis nodded her head in agreement as a smile turned up the corners of her lips. She felt a measure of satisfaction that her observations had been verified by the Doctor.

"Did you happen to notice his left arm where the IV needle was?" she asked.

"Yes," he replied. "I did, and it's truly unbelievable! The needle mark and the redness are completely gone. There is no sign of bruising either!"

He shook his head from side to side, scratched his head and laughed.

He said, "I cannot explain this from a medical viewpoint. It's sort of spooky, don't you think? Maybe he's just a superfast healer!"

Again, he gave a little laugh to hide his emotions.

She gave him a knowing look.

"It's really more like a miracle, don't you agree?" she said.

Now Doctor Hollis chuckled.

"Let's just wait for the x-rays. Remember, Nurse, this is strictly between the two of us, all right? It wouldn't do for this sort of thing to get out. There may be a reasonable explanation, but we'll have to wait and see. You know, something like this could turn this hospital into a three-ring circus! Why, we'd be up to our ears in reporters!" he stated.

He grimaced and shrugged his shoulders at the thought.

Her laughter fell musically on his ears.

"OK, Doctor, mum's the word. We'll keep this between the two of us. In the meantime, I'll keep a close eye on David Michaels," she responded.

He smiled warmly at her.

"I'm going out for a bite to eat and a little fresh air. I should be back in an hour or so. I'll check in by phone just in case of emergency. Besides, those x-rays might be complete. Curiosity is really gnawing on my mind now," he said.

He turned and walked down the hallway towards the elevators.

"Hold down the fort, trooper," he said over his shoulder as he chuckled again.

Nurse Lewis phoned the x-ray lab and left the instructions he had given her.

"Oh, boy," she mused while cradling the phone. "I can't wait to see those x-ray results!"

She busied herself at the Nurse's Station in preparation for her own shift change. She saw the technician from the x-ray lab bring up the machine so he could take the x-rays as requested. After a few minutes, he left. She was nearing the end of her shift, and Doctor Hollis still had not come back, nor had the results of the x-rays come up.

Small waves of curiosity and excitement washed over her. She found herself lingering around the Nurse's Station even after being relieved. For one reason or another, neither Doctor Hollis nor the x-ray results appeared.

"That stinker!" she smiled. "He's intentionally going to make me wait until tomorrow."

Reaching for her handbag, she turned, said goodnight to her relief crew, and left the floor.

CHAPTER 9

Nurse Lewis was in the parking lot, walking towards her car when she heard her name being called.

"Hey! Nurse Lewis!"

She stopped and turned to see Doctor Hollis trotting towards her.

He came to a stop a few feet from her and spoke, "I'm sorry I missed you at the Nurse's Station, but I'm glad I caught you before you left. Would you like to grab a cup of coffee so we can talk?"

"That would be nice," she replied with a smile turning up the corners of her mouth.

Together, they walked down the street and entered Tony's Restaurant, which sat on a corner. Nothing was said until coffee had been served.

Betty could not contain her curiosity any longer as she leaned forward against the booth table.

"Well, Doctor?" she asked with an eager, expectant expression on her face.

Doctor Hollis looked into her eyes and inhaled a long breath.

He said, "I can't explain it, Nurse. I've never seen anything like it! You called it a miracle, and you might be more right than you know because a miracle is as good a description as any I can offer!"

Betty took a quick, short breath and waited patiently.

"There's more to this," she thought.

Doctor Hollis took a sip of coffee and swallowed.

He continued, "You would have to see the x-rays to truly understand what I am saying. Both of David's leg bones are fused so perfectly that there's no evidence that they were ever broken! The x-rays of his ribs are the same—no signs of fractures! It's like David was never even involved in an accident in the first place! But I'm a lot like you, Nurse Lewis. I believe what my eyes tell me. Just between the two of us, I don't know why he's even in the hospital right now since there's nothing wrong with him! We could safely release him tonight!"

Nurse Lewis gasped in surprise as she thought, "I knew something marvelous was taking place! I just didn't know what to think about it! Nothing in my training or experience has prepared me for such an occurrence! It's mind boggling, and Doctor Hollis just verified with the x-rays that this is, indeed, a miracle!"

Out loud, Betty stated, "We know that the original x-rays were taken when he was brought to the Emergency Room, revealing the compound breaks in his legs."

Doctor Hollis responded, "Oh, we have both the before and after x-rays to prove the changes. The problem is…who would believe it anyway?"

Both of them sat in silence drinking their coffee as the enormity of this new information sank into both their minds…minds that were trained in the medical profession and the impossibility of the subject at hand.

After a few moments, Betty looked at Doctor Hollis and posed a point-blank question, "Do you think he healed himself? I know I do because I watched him rub his arm. The puncture mark and redness on his arm disappeared immediately! If he did heal himself, how did he accomplish it? Where could he possibly get that kind of knowledge and power?"

The questions tumbled out as she watched his face, waiting for a response.

He said, "Nurse, quite frankly, I'm stumped. I have no idea what to make of it. Think about this for a moment. If he can heal like this, he'll put me out of business because I can't compete!"

She replied, "There's one more question we might consider—as bad as I hate to even mention it—but do you think our patient might be an alien in disguise?"

Doctor Hollis gave her a pained expression, aghast at the mere words she had just spoken.

She quickly added, "I know it sounds far-fetched, but there has to be some sort of logical explanation."

"Well," Doctor Hollis stated, "I certainly can't do what he's apparently able to do, and I don't know of another doctor or machine that can perform such a feat. His legs look like they were never broken fourteen days ago!"

Betty nodded in agreement.

Doctor Hollis continued, "One thing I do know for sure, and that is we must keep all of this quiet at all costs. I can't begin to imagine what would happen if this got out and made the news."

"Just for the sake of conversation, let's agree that he does have the power to work these miracles," injected Betty. "He sure could do a whole lot of good for people. Who knows, maybe he would be willing to teach some of us?"

Doctor Hollis glanced at his watch, and then smiled at Nurse Lewis.

He thought, "I enjoy talking with her, but I just never seem to have enough time."

Aloud, he said, "I have to get back to the hospital, but before I go, I want to change the subject for a moment. We've worked together for a couple of years now, and we already know each other's first names. It seems to me that we could be less formal, especially when we're away from the hospital. How about it? All of my friends just call me Dan."

Betty smiled and said, "Why that's very nice, Dan. Actually, everyone calls me either Betty or Bet. I answer to both...just don't call me late for dinner," she joked.

"That's great," replied Dan. "Look, I've still got a couple of things to finish at the hospital before my head can touch a pillow," as he paid for the coffee. "Can I walk you back to your car?"

"Sure," she said, smiling.

They left Tony's and walked back toward the hospital staff parking lot. They chatted, mostly small talk, as they approached her car.

"Good night, Bet!" Dan said, turning to make his way back inside the hospital.

Betty smiled as she clicked her seatbelt into place and started her car.

She thought, "You know, girl, he's such a good-looking man," as she pulled out of the parking lot and headed home.

Continuing the thread of their conversation in her mind, she thought, "David is truly a mystery, yet he seems like a very nice but average kind of young man. This situation is very exciting and unusual for me. I've seen many trying times in my years of nursing. I've experienced joy and heartbreak with various patients, but nothing like this! I'm looking forward to tomorrow with eager anticipation!"

She spoke softly to herself like a little girl hoarding an Earth-shattering secret and said, "Just think, only David, Doctor Dan Hollis, and I know about this amazing miracle," and then she chuckled.

Betty parked her car, a dark green Ford sedan, in her garage and let herself into the kitchen through an adjoining door. From long habit, she hooked her purse strap over the back of a dining room chair.

Next, she went down the hallway into the bathroom and tripped the stopper on the bathtub. She turned on the hot and cold water, adjusting the temperature to her liking. While the tub was filling, she added her favorite lavender bubble bath powder to the water, giving it a swirl with her hand before she turned off the water. She then went back to the kitchen and prepared herself a large mug of hot tea. Carefully, she carried her tea to the small table at the side of the bathtub.

She dimmed the bathroom lights and undressed, thinking, "This is one of my favorite times, taking a long, hot, and soothing bath."

She smiled at the soft reflection of herself in the mirrored tub enclosure. What she saw was a very trim body of a thirty-year-old woman. She stood five feet seven inches tall barefooted. Even at her age, her breasts were still ample and erect. Her slim waist gave way to shapely hips and thighs. Her legs were well developed and muscular. She had blonde, shoulder-length hair with blondish-brown eyebrows, which were arched over wide set, large blue eyes that were separated by a pert up-turned nose. Her mouth completed the package with full, heart-shaped, pouting lips.

Betty was not vain nor did she suffer from delusions of false modesty. She was well aware of how men looked at her on the sly.

"Not too bad, not bad at all, for my age," she said, chuckling as she stepped into the tub and settled into the warm bubbly water.

She closed her eyes, letting the cares of the day evaporate.

"Now Dan would sure be a fine catch for some lucky lady!" she said, smiling at the thought, as well as the friendliness of using his first name.

CHAPTER 10

David tossed, turned and fidgeted as he lay back on the bed. He was having trouble getting comfortable and desperately wanted to take his legs down from the slings which held them elevated. The temptation to lower them was almost overpowering. He wanted to stand up and, better yet, walk on his own two feet. David was seriously considering lifting them out of the slings just for a few minutes when Doctor Hollis entered his room.

"Good morning, David," he spoke cheerfully as he approached the bedside.

He placed his stethoscope on David's chest and listened a few moments. Then he checked his vital signs.

He thought, "Bet is right—his vital signs really are normal!"

He said aloud, "How do you feel today?"

"I feel just fine, Doctor," replied David.

Doctor Hollis looked down at David's face, which held no sign of pain at all.

"I've got a lab technician bringing up a wheel chair to get you. He'll take you to the prosthetics lab and remove these leg casts. You know, it's miraculous, but our x-rays reveal that your ribs and legs are healed completely. In fact, they're perfectly normal again. I'll bet those casts are really uncomfortable for you."

"They sure are, Doctor, and the worst part is, when my legs itch, I can't scratch them!" David said, grinning.

Doctor Hollis said, "You know, I've seen a lot of things during my career—many wonderful things and some hard to believe—but I can't remember anything as marvelous as the complete cures on your legs and ribs! Could you tell me anything about how this happened?"

David felt his nerves go on edge, but he smiled bravely. He liked Doctor Hollis a lot, but his memory of Miranda's warning instruction registered a mental alarm.

He responded, "I haven't a clue, Doctor, but, like you, I think it must truly be a miracle!"

Doctor Hollis thought as he returned David's smile, shaking his head from side to side, "Here's one very smooth, intelligent young man. There's no possible explanation other than that he healed himself! Yet, David possesses the calm self discipline to agree with me instead of offering an outright but flat denial. I know now that any attempt to browbeat this young man is completely out of the question!"

Aloud, he said, "After the casts have been removed, David, the technician will bring you back here. I'll call your Mom and let her know how much better you are doing."

"That will be cool, Doctor Hollis. Thank you very much," said David.

At that moment, the laboratory technician entered the room, pushing a wheel chair.

"You sent for me, Doctor Hollis. Is this the one?" he indicated David by pointing his thumb.

"Yes, it is, John," replied Doctor Hollis as he reached up and began removing the slings from David's legs.

"Here, let me help with that," replied John as they gently lowered David's legs to the bed.

"David, you've been lying flat for a long time, so I want you to sit up carefully. You'll probably feel a little dizzy for a few minutes, but that's normal. Remember, when the casts are off, you'll have to be careful when you stand up," said Doctor Hollis.

Then he added, "John, after you remove his casts, I'd appreciate it if you'd just bring him back here in the wheel chair. We don't want any accidents occurring with patients under our care, now do we?" he said, winking at David as he spoke.

John, who was well-muscled, lifted David by placing one arm around his back and his other arm under the knee and sat him in the wheel chair.

"I'll take good care of him, Doctor Hollis. Come on, and let's see if this machine will peel rubber!" he said as he laughed and wheeled David out of the room and down the hallway.

In the meantime, Doctor Hollis completed his rounds, checking his other patients on the ward. In the process, he approached the Nurse's Station.

"Good morning, Nurse Lewis. How are you this fine morning?" he asked.

Betty looked up with a sweet smile and said, "Oh, good morning, Doctor. How are all our charges doing this morning?"

What she most wanted to ask was about one patient in particular, but Doctor Hollis had already guessed her unspoken question.

He said, "I've sent him down to prosthetics to have his casts removed. It's silly to make him wear casts and lay there in traction when it's unnecessary. Oh, by the way, I asked him if he knew how such a cure could happen. You know what he said? He told me that he had no clue and that it must truly be a miracle! Ha! I think he knows more than he's telling us, but he's certainly not going to confide in us. He's one very smart young man."

Nurse Lewis looked at the Doctor, her face mirroring her wonderment.

"That's strange," she replied. "He looks so normal—just your average boy. I still wonder where he would get such power and knowledge to heal like that and what else might he be able to do?"

Doctor Hollis' forehead was wrinkled in thought, but before he could frame an answer, he heard laughter coming from the hallway. John was pushing David along briskly and both were laughing hardily. Doctor Hollis could not help smiling when he heard them.

He moved towards them as he spoke, "Just wheel him back into Room 110, John."

Once David was safely inside his room, John looked at Doctor Hollis and said, "Do you want me to wait and then take the wheel chair with me, Doc?"

"No, we might still need it for a little while," replied Doctor Hollis. "I'll either give you a call or have one of the aides bring it down when we're finished with it."

"OK, Doc," replied John as he playfully faked a punch to David's shoulder before pivoting towards the door. "Take it easy, David, and drop by the lab to say hello."

"I will if I get the chance," replied David, smiling.

"Well, David, let's see if you can stand," said Doctor Hollis, "but first, let's get a little help," as he pushed the nurse's call button.

Almost immediately, Nurse Lewis entered the room. She had watched John push David's wheel chair back to his room. Her burning curiosity had compelled her to go there unrequested.

As she came into the room, she smiled and said, "You rang?"

Doctor Hollis returned her smile, thinking, "I like her personality."

Aloud, he said, "Grab hold of David's right arm," as he took the left side. "Let's see if this young man can stand."

With Doctor Hollis on one side and Nurse Lewis on the other, David leaned forward from the wheel chair and began to gingerly place his weight on his feet.

Doctor Hollis stated, "As I said before, you'll be a little dizzy, David."

David did feel dizzy, and his legs felt shaky, but there was no pain in his legs or ribs. He was glad Doctor Hollis and Nurse Lewis were there to help support him. Slowly, the dizzy spell passed, and the shakiness left his legs. Tentatively, he lifted his left foot and moved it forward in a small step.

He thought, "Still, there's no pain!" as he placed his weight on his left foot, moving his right foot up even with his left, completing his first step.

After several steps, Doctor Hollis nodded to Nurse Lewis, saying, "That's enough for right now."

Together, they assisted David back to the wheel chair and helped him sit back down. They noticed small beads of sweat had popped out on David's forehead and lower lip.

"That was great, David, but we don't want to over-do it the first time," said Doctor Hollis, "Don't worry. It's just going to take a little time, but you'll get stronger with each session. Why, you'll be walking normal in no time at all!"

Nurse Lewis nodded in agreement as she beamed at David.

Doctor Hollis said, "You did just great, and you know what? I'll bet you a donut you'll be walking unassisted up and down this hallway by this time tomorrow. But right now, I want you to rest for a little while in that chair, and Nurse Lewis will send a couple of aides to help you walk some more a little later."

As he left, he motioned for Nurse Lewis to accompany him. They left together. Neither one spoke until they were at the Nurse's Station.

"Well," he said, "what do you think?"

"It's truly unbelievable, Doctor Hollis. I wouldn't have believed it if I hadn't seen it with my very own eyes!" she stated.

"My sentiments, exactly!" smiled Doctor Hollis. "There are some strange but wonderful, inexplicable things which happen in this old world. It sure makes a person wish for more knowledge…at least, it does me."

Nurse Lewis gave him an understanding look of empathy.

"What do we do now, Doctor?" she asked.

"The only thing we can do: Get him walking without assistance and release him. When he's walking well, I'll call his mother to pick him up. I mean, it's silly to keep him here when he's recovered completely! No one would believe us, Nurse Lewis. Why butt our heads into a brick wall?" he replied.

Just then, the phone rang and Nurse Lewis answered it. After listening for a moment, she handed the receiver to Doctor Hollis.

She watched him nod his head and utter a comment, and then finished by saying, "I'll be right there."

He hung up the phone and nodded to her.

"Got to run. Duty calls. That was the Emergency Room. See you later," he spoke over his shoulder as he disappeared at a fast trot down the hallway.

CHAPTER 11

The ambulance had barely come to a complete stop before the Emergency Medical Team was opening the doors and rolling a patient into the Emergency Room.

Doctor Hollis could see the patient was a young female wearing both arm and leg braces, and she was having trouble breathing. Working quickly and listening to the EMT, Doctor Hollis assisted Doctor Albert Winston with getting the young patient on a bed. Several tests later, it was revealed that the young girl had Pneumonia. She was placed in an oxygen tent.

Doctor Hollis thought, "The EMT had already started an IV on her. In a short period of time in the Emergency Room, she'll hopefully stabilize enough to be moved up to a room. She's in a weakened condition, but her vital signs aren't bad, considering she has Polio."

Looking at her through the oxygen tent, he thought, "Actually, she's a lovely girl, with a harmonious-sounding name: Melody Ann Prescott."

Doctor Winston looked at Doctor Hollis, grinned and said, "I think she'll be OK,

Dan. We just have to keep a close check on her vitals. That girl has a lot of heart, and she's been fighting an uphill battle."

He responded, "That's great news, Al. She deserves a break. I'm going back up to the ward now. You know how it is—always busy. Will you bring her up, or do you want one of our nurse's aides to come down for her?"

"Oh, don't worry. I'll have her brought up," replied Doctor Winston. "By the way, is our golf game still on for day after tomorrow?"

"You bet," Doctor Hollis said with a laugh. "It'll be wonderful to get out, enjoy some sun and hit a few balls."

Doctor Hollis made his way to the elevators and pushed the up button.

He thought, "I enjoy golf a lot. I play every chance I can get, which just isn't often enough! Al's a much better golfer than I am, but I enjoy the camaraderie, plus the friendly competition."

As the elevator came to a stop and the doors opened, he had a random thought, "I wonder if Betty Lewis plays golf? I know I would enjoy her company. Maybe later, I'll ask her to satisfy my curiosity. Who am I kidding?" He smiled to himself. "Every time I'm near her, there's an undercurrent of magnetic attraction. My heart beats faster, and I feel lighter. Let's face it," he chided himself, "she excites me. I enjoy being around her, even if I do try to not show it publicly."

Doctor Hollis walked up to the Nurse's Station and motioned to Nurse Lewis to come over.

"Nurse Lewis, we have a new patient coming up shortly from the Emergency Room, and she'll need a room," he said.

Briefly, he filled her in on the patient's status and requirements.

She turned and went over to two nurse's aides, quickly briefing them. They left to prepare a room.

He continued, "Doctor Winston and I think she'll be just fine, but we'll have to monitor her closely for awhile."

Meanwhile, David had observed the nurse's aides bustling about Room 112, which was adjacent to the room he was in.

He watched as they brought a patient to the room a short while later. The gurney was covered with an oxygen tent. He heard snatches of conversation concerning a young lady with both Pneumonia and Polio.

He wheeled himself past the Nurse's Station and into the lounge area to watch a little television before his next walking session began.

David could feel his strength returning to his body and knew he was going to be just fine.

He smiled as he thought, "I'll be released from the hospital soon, and I'll be able to help my Mom again."

CHAPTER 12

Maria and Josie, nurse's aides, each gripped one of David's arms.

"Ouch! Their grip is just a little too tight!" David thought with a nervous grin.

These nurse's aides were full of light-hearted teasing as they maneuvered David down the hall. He tried to concentrate on his foot placement, but it was not easy, flanked on each side by two attractive young ladies.

Before the trio reached Room 112, Josie spoke on impulse, "Let's stop by to see how our new patient is doing."

"Great!" stated Maria, as she began a turning motion and pulling on David's arm.

"It's not just their looks and teasing," he thought with a nervous smile, "but it's their closeness and scent. I've never been close to members of the opposite sex, but I like it a lot, indeed I do!"

Maria interrupted his thoughts with a mock serious command: "Stand up straight, Davey. You wouldn't want your girlfriend to see you slouching around, would you?"

Both of the aides were giggling by then, which made David's blush turn even redder.

He thought, "I haven't had any experience with girls, and I don't know what to say or how to react to this teasing."

Instead, he set his jaw firmly and suffered in silence, hoping they would not notice his uneasiness. He concentrated on his feet, putting one before the other, trying to stand erect.

Once inside the room, the threesome stopped so they could look inside the oxygen tent. Maria held a finger over her lips to signal silence, which was really an unnecessary gesture as the three silently gazed at the young face composed in an uneasy sleep.

David's breath caught in the back of his throat!

"I've never seen a more beautiful girl!" he thought as he gazed at the perfectly arched eyebrows and long eye lashes, as well as her peaches and cream complexion.

As if on cue, the aides nudged David. As quietly as possible, they eased out of the room and went into David's room, where he was deposited on his bed in a sitting position.

"You're doing very well, David, but why not rest awhile before trying it again?" stated Maria with a nice smile.

"OK," replied David, returning her smile, but his thoughts were still occupied with the female patient in Room 112.

"How can I go about helping her, away from prying eyes? Whatever I'm going to do will have to be completed in a short period of time because Doctor Hollis has already informed me that I will be released from the hospital tomorrow."

David checked off the possibilities in his mind and suddenly smiled as he thought, "My plan is simple enough, and I'll only need a short period of time to do it when there's the least amount of activity." David smiled in satisfaction, thinking, "It will work, of this I am certain."

CHAPTER 13

David had practiced walking and resting the rest of the day, finally eating his evening meal. He stayed in the lounge area, watching television impatiently as the minutes and hours seemed to drag on for an eternity. Finally, all the visitors had left and complete quiet descended on the ward. David had returned to his room, waiting for his chance.

It was one o'clock in the morning when David peeked around the doorway to his room, checking the hallway for any movement. There was none.

All was still as he stole into Room 112 and approached Melody's bedside.

"So far, so good," he thought, as his heart beat rapidly.

He gazed down at her face, which was composed in a fitful sleep. Her eyelids fluttered, and the corner of her mouth twitched as if she was in pain or experiencing an unpleasant dream.

Quickly, David concentrated as he began moving his hands back and forth, approximately two inches above Melody's covered legs and feet. He could feel the heat and energy flowing from his hands. When he was satisfied that the healing process on her legs and feet was complete, he gently raised the oxygen tent sides and placed his hands over her arms, beginning the same healing motion over her arms and hands. David intently watched her face for any signs of awakening. Finally, he moved his hands over her chest and smiled in satisfaction as he noticed the lip twitching and eyelid fluttering had ceased.

Very gently he lowered the tent's sides back into place, straightened the bed covers, and tucked her in. David took one last, long look at her face, now composed in a small smile. Her face was completely relaxed now, and David smiled too.

"Wow! She is indeed beautiful!" he thought as he turned and began easing towards the door.

Unknown to David, something just then had caused Melody to awaken and open her eyes. Perhaps it was her subconscious, recognizing an absence of the pain which she had constantly experienced since she had become ill with Polio years before. Suddenly, she felt no pain and had no difficulty with her breathing.

She could see the back of a male through the clear plastic of her oxygen tent. He was leaving the room.

She experienced an impulse to call out to him, but was not certain whether she was awake or asleep, dreaming it all. So she did nothing.

Melody was always fully aware of her health condition so she thought, "Maybe the doctors gave me some pain medicine—that would explain why I feel no pain."

On impulse, she raised her right arm and immediately noticed: "I can do this without any pain at all!" Her breath caught in her throat as she thought, "Why I can see that my right hand is no longer gnarled—my fingers are relaxed and flexible!" Quickly, she looked at her left hand and thought, "Wow! It's the same, and I can move my left arm!"

Melody was in a mild state of shock.

"How could I move my arms and hands without pain?" she wondered.

She then glanced at her feet.

With her heart beating rapidly, she summoned her courage and said, "I'm going to try to wiggle my toes since I haven't been able to do that for years." Adding to her complete wonderment, she sang, "Glory be to God! My toes on both feet are responding to my mental commands!"

There was no explaining the excitement which completely engulfed her at this glorious moment in time.

However, just as quickly as the exhilaration filled her, it was replaced by cold, icy fingers of dread gripping her heart and mind.

"Oh, God!" she moaned in a broken voice. "Please don't let this be temporary! Please don't give me this wonderful ability to move without pain and then take it away!" she pleaded. "Please don't let this be just a dream!"

The minutes turned into hours as Melody moved one member after the other.

She just kept thinking, "Even though my arms and legs are still encased in my braces, I can move them! I think I could remove the braces, but I really don't think that's a good idea, not yet anyway! I can only marvel at how wonderful and intricate are my arms, hands, fingers, legs, ankles, feet and toes! Most people take these for granted! They just do not appreciate what they have or how fortunate they are—they can move freely and without pain!"

Melody glanced at the clock in her room and smiled. It was 4:30 in the morning and her eye lids were getting heavy again.

She thought, "I am almost afraid to close my eyes for fear that, when I wake up, I will be encased again in the same old, paralyzed, limited-movement, pain-filled body. Maybe I should call for a nurse and share my wonderful news! No, maybe I should wait until later this morning. I need to get some sleep. When I wake up, there will be ample time to share the news—especially if I am cured, and this isn't all just a wonderful dream after all!"

Before falling asleep, she wanted to give thanks. She tried to frame her words of gratitude and praise. She had so many things she wanted to say, but sleep overtook her first.

She did manage to mumble, "Thank you, God, for this wonderful gift!"

CHAPTER 14

David was awakened by the noise coming from Room 112. It was only 7:30 in the morning, but already there was a beehive-like activity in the hallway as nurses and doctors came and went from the adjoining room.

David finished his breakfast as he tried to pick out the different voices coming from the room next to him. He was sure he recognized Nurse Lewis' voice, and there was no mistaking Maria's musically infectious laugh. He thought he also recognized Doctor Hollis' voice. There were excited exchanges and exclamations, mixed with laughter, which brought a smile to David's face, along with a deeper feeling of immense satisfaction.

"It's truly wonderful to be able to help someone!" he thought.

David's thoughts were suddenly interrupted by Doctor Hollis and Nurse Lewis, who entered his room and approached his bed. Doctor Hollis wore a serious expression while Nurse Lewis' face bore a small smile.

Doctor Hollis spoke, "Good morning, David. How are you doing this morning?"

"I'm doing fine, Doctor Hollis, and my ability to walk has improved a lot. In fact, you owe me a donut already! Actually, I was just about to walk next door to see what all the excitement is about. I can hear the laughter and voices," David responded.

Now Nurse Lewis spoke, "So you don't know what's happened? Why it appears that we have another remarkable miracle on our hands. Your fellow patient, Melody Ann Prescott, came into the hospital with both Pneumonia and Polio, with braces on both legs and arms. Somehow, during the night, she experienced a healing miracle, or should I say miracles? Both the Pneumonia and Polio are gone!"

Doctor Hollis watched David's face very closely as Nurse Lewis continued with the amazing news. He was watching for any tell tale sign, a nervous reaction, something, anything, that David knew or was in some way involved, but there was no indication on his face of anything other than a little smile.

"So that's her name," thought David, "a pretty name for a beautiful girl."

"Her lungs are clear, and she has full motion and flexibility in both arms and legs. We have removed her braces as she no longer needs them! Maria and Josie are going to begin walking her around a little to strengthen her legs. We'll also introduce other exercises to strengthen her arms and upper torso as well. It'll take some time, but she should be up and around in no time. It's truly amazing…in fact, unbelievable…even impossible!" reflected Nurse Lewis, catching her breath.

"Wow!" stated David, smiling, "so that's what all the noise is about. I think it's great, and I'm happy for her. You know, Doctor Hollis, you're going to be flooded with patients when others find out about these miracles happening here. Everyone is going to want one!"

He finished with another smile and the most innocent look he could manage.

"I know, I know, and that's what bothers me!" said Doctor Hollis in a tone of resignation.

To himself, he thought, "This young man, sitting on the bed in front of us, is either completely innocent, as he claims, or he is one very evasive individual. What's happened here during the last week is not only unbelievable, but it's turned medical knowledge upside down! It's baffled and teased us, tugging at the corners of the reality that we understand, giving a glimpse into the wonderful realm of the unknown."

Aloud, he said, "Well, David, you're as well as you can possibly be, so I'll have Nurse Lewis complete your discharge paperwork. Tonight you'll be able to sleep in your own bed. I'll also call your Mom and give her the good news."

He extended his hand toward David, who shook the Doctor's hand.

"You're an amazing young man, David, and it's been a pleasure to know you," he said.

"Thank you, Doctor Hollis, for taking such good care of me," returned David. "That goes for you, too, Nurse Lewis. You guys have been just swell," he said with a smile.

Doctor Hollis and Nurse Lewis left David's room and strolled together to the Nurse's Station.

"You know, Doctor," Nurse Lewis said with a smile, "I don't know how these miracles happened, but I'm glad I was here when they occurred. I know it probably sounds sort of weird, but somehow it restores my faith. I mean, after all, everything that has happened has been wonderful!"

Doctor Hollis nodded his agreement as he replied, "It's too bad we couldn't find out how the miraculous cures happened, not once but twice in one week! I'll bet my bottom dollar that David knows more than he's telling, but there's no way we can force him to tell us."

"It is too bad we cannot get more information. We could do so much good with that kind of knowledge," sighed Nurse Lewis.

"By the way, Bet," smiled Doctor Hollis, using her first name informally as no one could hear, "Do you play golf?"

Betty could not contain herself as she laughed out loud. The sudden change in subjects, coupled with the look on his face, had caught her completely off balance.

"No, Dan," she said with another of her special smiles, looking up into that handsome face. "In fact, I wouldn't know a golf ball from a football. Why?"

"Because tomorrow, I have a golf outing scheduled with Doctor Winston and probably a couple of others. I just thought you might like to tag along," joked Dan light heartedly.

"Dan, are you asking me for a date?" teased Betty, flashing her smile at him, revealing her sparkling white teeth.

Her blue eyes danced mischievously.

"As a matter of fact, I am," said Dan, chuckling.

"OK, I think I'd enjoy the exercise and company, Dan, but I am telling you the truth when I said I don't know anything about golf," she stated.

"That's all right. You can just come along and keep me company. Later, we'll have lunch at the Clubhouse. Could I pick you up at your place...if you will give me your address...say around ten o'clock?" he asked, smiling.

"That would be just fine, Dan. Here, let me write my address down for you. It's easy to find. I'll be ready at ten," she responded.

"OK," said Doctor Hollis with a sigh. "Well, I guess it's back to the salt mines. I have more patients to check on...ones that don't have any miracles, that is. I'll see you later."

He spoke the last words over his shoulder as he was walking away.

He thought, "I also have to call David's Mom, Julie, and let her know that David is ready to be released from the hospital. I know she will be happy about that!"

CHAPTER 15

Curtis Youngblood was fifty-eight years old and did not look a day over forty-five. He was a millionaire several times over. Curtis took great pride in his ability as an entrepreneur in either finding a niche or creating one and then filling it. His car dealerships were getting larger each year because of his dynamic and aggressive business expansions.

Curtis thought, "I did not get to where I am by being a choir boy. No! No! I believe in always trying to be the first person with the most to offer, and rarely do I accept 'No' for an answer. When the situation demands it, I can be suave and polished, even charming. I can also be insistent, demanding and blunt. I know I possess a very mean temper, but I go to great efforts to conceal it. Rarely has anyone seen my dark side, which I expose only when I am completely alone."

He was deep in contemplation by then: "For all intents and purposes, most people know me as a good husband and father to my son, Nathan. There's not anything I wouldn't do for my son, who's eleven years old now. Nate, as I like to call him, has been skinny, frail and sickly from birth. For some reason, Nate just never seemed to flourish. I've taken him to doctor after doctor. Test after test has been conducted, and none of them could explain or even identify a problem area!" he thought in exasperation.

"Nate's just not like other young boys, either, in that he has no interest in any kind of outdoor sports. He just does not like to run or play normally, like other kids. Instead, he prefers to read, play indoor parlor games or draw. That just breaks my heart."

"At the same time, I am angry inside because I desperately want Nate to like sports, like baseball, football, soccer or even run track. To see my son sitting inside, looking pale, skinny, and sickly simply irritates me to no end!"

"Clare, my wife of fifteen years, and I have discussed Nate and his physical condition countless times. Both of us are very active during our leisure time. She enjoys swimming, and my favorite outdoor past time is golfing. We are both baffled by Nathan's apparent dislike for anything that requires muscular activity!"

"Thinking about golf," Curtis said aloud as he turned to look at his calendar schedule. "Sure enough, I'm set up to golf with Doctor Winston at 10:30 tomorrow morning. Good!"

Curtis was sitting in his favorite recliner in the family room.

He glanced toward the kitchen and raised his voice, "Clare, Dear, would you like to golf a few holes tomorrow?"

"No can do tomorrow, Curtis. Remember? It's Ladies League Bowling. Sorry," she said as she smiled at him when she came into the room.

"Oh, yeah, it slipped my mind," returned Curtis. Speaking to himself, he said, "I guess I had better go put my golf clubs in the trunk of my car while I am thinking about it. It will be good to get out on the course again. I enjoy Doctor Winston's company."

Rising, he made his way toward the hallway closet to retrieve his golf clubs.

CHAPTER 16

The healing process which David had used on himself had been closely monitored by Miranda, who had made detailed mental notes of the whole scenario.

She thought, "David made a simple blunder while healing himself because he was caught in the act by the nurse. Nevertheless, he did make an awkward but timely recovery. Hopefully, he'll get better with practice."

Miranda laughed when she thought, "I wonder what David would say about his close call, which was definitely not cool."

"Before David came to Gorbandihar, He Who Summons also informed me that He wished to be briefed on David's training progress and, of course, on his efforts in using the healing techniques. I've already briefed Him on the situation, including his little ordeal with Nurse Betty Lewis."

Thinking about that, Miranda smiled again.

"I've never experienced mental laughter coming from He Who Summons before, but it certainly was then!"

Thinking about the situation brought another nice smile to Miranda's lovely face.

"Everybody likes David very much, and one thing I did not tell him, either during his training or after, is the simple fact that He Who Summons cares very deeply and will be very watchful of any pain or harm coming to him from any quarter! The Earth is such a strange place—it is a mixture of good and bad in so many ways."

Reaching out, Miranda flipped a few switches and made some fine frequency adjustments to a couple of dials before rising from her command chair.

"I have to hurry! Another briefing is due on David's healing progress with Melody Ann, and I don't want to be late! It's strange, in a way, because I am positive that He Who Summons already knows all about David. Still, for whatever reason, He wants timely briefings from me."

"Not only that, but I'm not the only one making briefings, as they go on continuously from so many others. I do look forward to these briefings because it is so enjoyable, just being in the presence of He Who Summons. For some reason, I not only feel better, but the light always seems so much brighter!"

CHAPTER 17

David was sitting on his bed, thinking about Melody, when the phone rang, interrupting his thoughts.

"Hello," David said, cradling the phone on his shoulder.

"David, it's Mom," Julie responded on the other end. "Doctor Hollis just got off the phone with me. He says you can be released now! That is so amazing! I don't understand how it could possibly be true, after all you've been through, but I'm sure the power of prayer has played a part! I am so excited! Dr. Hollis suggested that I bring you a change of clothes because the ones you had on at the time of the accident are all soiled and torn up. Anything special you want me to bring?"

"Yes, Mom, could you bring me a pair of jeans, a shirt, and regular underclothes? My tennis shoes should be all right," David spoke into the receiver.

"OK, Son. I've got to go by the house to get your stuff, but I should be there in an hour or so. I can't tell you how happy I am!" she exclaimed.

"I'm happy, too, Mom. It'll be good to get home and back to normal," David replied.

She said, "I love you, David. I'll see you soon."

"OK," he responded.

David had no way of knowing that his life would never really be normal again, or return to what had been normal before the accident.

He arose from the bed and began walking down the hallway. As he came abreast of the doorway to Room 112, he stopped and peered inside.

Melody was next to the bed, holding herself up in a standing position, using a walker. Her knees were bent and shaking a little because the muscle structure in her legs was not developed due to being confined to a wheel chair for so many years, being unable to move either her arms or legs.

Her face was flushed red and bore a fine sheen of sweat due to her efforts. She had not noticed David's presence because of her concentration.

"Hi!" David said with a big smile. "I'm David Michaels, your neighbor from Room 110. How's it going?"

Melody looked up in surprise.

"Oh, hello, I'm Melody Ann Prescott," she said.

David moved over to her side and helped her gain a sitting position on the bed.

"Thanks a lot," she said, breathing heavily.

"It's all right," returned David, taking a seat in one of two chairs present. "I heard about your good fortune. I couldn't help hearing all the commotion this morning. To see you actually standing after all you've been through is truly wonderful! I guess miracles really do happen," he continued.

Melody caught her breath and responded, "It is definitely a miracle for me, but I have found standing and walking—even taking little baby steps—is hard work! It looks so easy when you watch someone else doing it. I mean, it looks so natural, but when you haven't done it for such a long time, that's another thing all together! Still," she said, laughing with the excitement of it all, "I just know I'll get the hang of it!"

"Sure, you will! Why I'll bet that, in a few days, you'll not only be walking, but you'll even be dancing if you want to!" he spoke encouragingly.

"I don't know about the dancing part," she said, laughing.

David thought, "Her laughter sounds like bells tinkling happily. I don't remember any other girl who sounds like she does!"

They continued to pass the time, laughing and talking, without realizing how much time had gone by.

Suddenly, Julie poked her head into the room and said, "I thought I recognized your voice," she said, smiling at David as she continued on into the room.

"Mom, I want you to meet Melody Ann Prescott," David spoke gently.

Julie stepped forward and took one of Melody's hands and said softly, "I'm very pleased to meet you, Melody."

"I'm pleased to meet you, Mrs. Michaels," Melody responded.

"Oh, just call me Julie, please. Mrs. Michaels sounds too formal to me," she said.

Julie turned to David and said, "Well, David, I put the bag with your clothing in it on your bed. If you'll get dressed, I'll go sign the release forms so we can be on our way. I'm sorry I can't stay and visit longer, but I have to get back to work," she said, smiling at Melody as she finished speaking.

"OK, Mom," David replied as he rose and made his way out of the door, followed by Julie, who waved in a small friendly gesture to Melody as she left the room.

Melody's right hand came up involuntarily to her throat in amazement. Her heart skipped a beat as she looked at the back of David's head and back!

She thought, "His profile and the way he walks are exactly like the person who was inside my room last night. I wasn't dreaming after all! Why, it wasn't a miracle all by itself! It certainly had some help! Now I know the truth!"

She felt like shouting out loud, but something inside told her to be still and calm.

She thought, "After all, I can obtain his address or telephone number at the Nurse's Station, maybe a phone book, or perhaps through the school."

An enchanting smile played at the corners of her mouth.

"David Michaels, you have not seen the last of Melody Ann Prescott!" she stated emphatically.

This thought made the blood creep up towards her ears.

About thirty minutes later, David and his Mom, Julie, reappeared in her room.

"We just wanted to say good bye and wish you luck, as well as a speedy recovery, before we leave," said David.

"That's right," Julie said with a smile. "We hope you'll get well soon. We are very concerned about you, young lady!"

"Oh, thank you both so much," said Melody, beaming. "I just know I'm going to be walking really well very soon!"

"Well, we must run, Son, because I really do have to get back to work," replied Julie, as she turned to go out the door.

David had a hard lump in his throat as he smiled and made a small gesture with his right hand before leaving the room. He just could not speak at that moment. He was overcome with a feeling of loss, knowing that it was likely he would never see Melody again. The finality of it all left an empty hole inside of him.

CHAPTER 18

Dan picked Betty up and drove to the Denver Country Club. On the way, he looked at her and thought, "I can't help but notice how she chose a light blue blouse, which compliments her shining blonde hair, which in turn frames and highlights her blue eyes. I am going to have to be careful! It would be so easy to lose myself completely in the depths of those eyes."

Aloud, he said with a smile, "Wow, Bet, you look as fresh and pretty as a Morning Glory this morning!"

"Why, Dan, I do believe you're waxing poetic on me," she said as she laughed gaily.

Secretly, she was bubbling inside because of his attention and compliment.

When they arrived, he opened the door for her and then opened the trunk to retrieve his golf bag. He could already feel the sun shining warmly on his shoulders as he hefted the clubs.

"Sure looks like we're going to have a great day for golfing," he remarked, glancing at the clear blue skies.

As they entered the door of the Country Club, Dan spotted Al Winston and his wife, Jessica. They were with two gentlemen Dan did not know. They moved over to the small group, and Al made the introductions to a car dealer named Curtis Youngblood and one of his salesmen named Art.

"Curtis can set you up with a great buy if you're in the market, Dan, but watch him carefully or he'll have you in a Cadillac when all you wanted to buy was a Chevy," Al said with a chuckle.

Betty and Jessica laughed, too, at Al's joking manner.

"Did Curtis teach you to sell cars, Art?" teased Jessica.

"He taught me everything I know," replied Art with a big smile, "but he didn't teach me anything about golf. I hope you guys don't beat me too badly."

"You'll do fine, Art," returned Curtis smoothly. "Besides, it's just a friendly game. What say we get started everyone?"

"That suits me to a tee," said Dan, laughing. "It's been so long since I've played.

I'll probably need coaching on which club to use!"

"What's a club?" asked Betty with a smile.

The whole group was laughing and in good humor as they engaged five caddies to carry the golf bags.

The morning was progressing along incredibly well. Betty was beginning to understand why people enjoyed golfing so much.

They were on the seventh tee when Al asked Dan, "How's that Polio patient, Melody Ann Prescott, doing?"

Caught off guard, Dan said, "Surely you've heard, Al—she is healed!"

Al responded with surprise, "This is a jest, isn't it, Dan? Melody has been in that condition for years!"

"No, Al, it's true! We don't understand how it happened either, but it did!" said Dan, who then continued and explained about David Michaels' cure from the car accident injuries as well.

They were totally caught up in their conversation, unaware of anyone else or where they were.

Dan watched Al's eyes grow big in astonishment.

"That's impossible!" said Al, snorting in disbelief.

Neither Dan nor Al noticed Curtis' eyes narrowing as he digested this amazing information. Already, ideas began to form in his crafty mind.

He thought, "This information could be a veritable gold mine! Just imagine how I could use this!"

Dan continued, "I know it sounds crazy, Al, but I have before and after x-rays of David's legs and ribs. Betty here has seen them, too."

Al looked at Betty expectantly.

"Dan's right," Betty responded, quietly. Then she explained about what had happened to David's arm.

Al shook his head, and said, "I've never heard of anything like this before!"

"Wait a minute, guys," piped in Jessica. "We're here to play golf—not talk shop. So how about it, huh?"

"OK, OK, Darling. You're right," Al said with a smile. "Let's finish the course, but when we're through, Dan, I want to hear more about this, OK?"

"You've got it!" said Dan.

He glanced at Betty and slowly shook his head. He knew he had completely forgotten himself and where they were. She simply shrugged her shoulders because she understood how both of them had inadvertently let the cat out of the bag about David and Melody.

Later, after they had lunch at the Clubhouse, they were in the car and on their way back to Betty's house.

Dan spoke, "Dad-gummit! I started speaking without even thinking, Bet. I hope we didn't blow it too badly!"

She placed her hand on Dan's arm as they arrived at her home.

"Maybe Curtis and Art won't mention it or say anything," she said. "If worse comes to worse, we'll just deal with it as best we can. Now, if you won't think me forward, I'll invite you in for something cold to drink, or maybe put on a fresh pot of coffee," she smiled, teasingly.

"You don't have to ask me twice," quipped Dan, returning her smile.

He unsnapped his seat belt and quickly went around to open the door for her.

"What I'd really like is a tall, cold glass of iced tea, if you have any," he said, laughing.

"Oh, I think I can come up with a glass of tea," she responded as they both went into her neat kitchen.

Dan seated himself at her dining table.

He thought, "I enjoy watching her easy, graceful movements as she moves about making our tea. Easy boy," he chided himself, "Take it easy!"

Betty glanced over her shoulder and smiled at Dan. Her smile was warm and genuine.

"It's good to have such a handsome man sitting at my table. He seems to be completely relaxed," she thought. "It's such a comfortable feeling, with Dan just sitting there, returning my smile."

CHAPTER 19

Curtis Youngblood hung up the phone and smiled broadly to himself, thinking, "Money can buy so many things—so many different kinds of services, if one knows where to look! The price was high, but, if all goes well, my money will be well spent! David Michaels will be kidnapped and brought to my secret location unharmed, where he will be kept secure until he successfully heals my son, Nate! I don't have to worry about consequences if I'm caught. After all, I have many influential friends. All I would have to do is call in some markers—as a last resort, of course."

Curtis laughed out loud.

"This is really going to be easy," he thought as he left his study and went into the kitchen.

"Clare, you mentioned wanting to visit your mother and shop in Los Angeles while you are out there. Do you still want to go?" he asked.

Clare let out a little squeal of pleasure.

"Do you really mean it, Curtis? I could take Nathan, and Mom would be so happy to see us both," she stated.

Well," Curtis spoke thoughtfully, "I was hoping that Nate and I could have a little father-son time together while you are gone, you know, maybe take in a ball game, boy stuff. Besides, it'll do you good to get a breather from us guys. You and your Mom can go shopping and do girl stuff."

Curtis smiled as he did his very best selling job.

After a few moments, Clare looked at Curtis and said, "Are you sure you two will be all right? After all, a week is a long time. What will you guys eat?"

"Aw, Clare, don't you worry about us. We can always go out somewhere or have pizza brought in," he laughed. "Seriously, we'll be just fine."

Clare came over and gave Curtis a big hug and kiss.

"I'll take you up on your offer if you're sure you two will be OK," she said.

Curtis returned her hug as he spoke in her ear, "We'll be just fine, Dear."

Curtis went into the living room and reclined back in his chair as he idly watched the television screen. It looked like he was watching the screen intently, but, in reality, his mind was on many other things.

He thought, "All the pieces are falling neatly into place in my plan. The kidnapping is ready for execution, and I have neatly gotten Clare out of the way. So far, so good! If all goes according to plan, and if this David Michaels is indeed a healer with power, then Clare might get a real surprise when she gets back from Los Angeles!"

He continued contemplating, "In the meantime, I hope to pull this little operation off as quickly and quietly as possible. Money is so very useful!"

CHAPTER 20

Lately, Julie had been experiencing pain in her chest area. Finally, she had asked Dr. Jacobson, a doctor whom she worked with, if he would do her a favor and check her out. Doctor Jacobson had readily agreed and had even taken several x-rays.

After receiving the results of the x-rays that morning, Doctor Jacobson had called Julie into his office.

"Julie," he said, "I don't know how to tell you this in anything other than a straight-forward manner—you have Lung Cancer!"

Julie sat there for a moment, trying to control her emotions, but it was of no avail as tears just flowed and she sobbed her heart out.

Doctor Jacobson did his best to console her, but Julie was so disheartened.

She finally stood up, straightened her hair and patted her uniform, lifted her chin and said, "I guess I'd best get back to work. I just need a moment to wash my face and get some composure back."

She thought, "Maybe, if I could just be busy, I could put on a brave front and just get through the day."

It had actually almost worked until she got home from work.

"That was three hours ago, and my nerves have settled down, just a little bit. When it rains, it pours!" she thought as tears continued to pour down her cheeks. "Maybe a long soothing soak will help. It certainly couldn't hurt, could it? In my present state of mind, who knows?"

She set about running a tub of hot water for herself. She looked in the mirror and saw her eyes were still red from crying so much. She then undressed and got into the tub.

Anxious thoughts just kept coming into her mind: "I just can't seem to get a break— first it was David and now it's me! What concerns me most is what will happen to David and how will I pay my medical bills? David is out of the hospital and back in school. Our life was just getting back to normal!"

"One thing is certain, David must not know about my little problem until I am unable to hide it any more. I don't want to worry him right now. He's in his senior year of high school and doing so well."

As she continued to consider her plight, she said aloud, "I need to stop crying all these tears and emphasizing the negative side of this situation! This will never change anything! One thing is certain. I've reached the bottom, so the only way left to go is up! I've always been an optimist, and I'm not going to change now!"

As she finally lay back, relaxing in the warm water, her frame of mind was already improving as her lips moved in a quiet prayer, asking for help.

CHAPTER 21

David was very surprised and pleased that Melody had called his School Administration Office, trying to locate him. He had gotten a message, asking him to call her back.

"I returned her call and spoke with her far longer than I realized. It was so nice to hear her voice and laughter," he thought. "Time just flew by!"

Now he was walking home. He did not notice the large white van which was tailing him. He was just whistling and carefree as he strolled along, thinking about his conversation with Melody.

Suddenly, a man looking in a window turned to follow behind David just as the van pulled up alongside the curb next to him. Before he could even sense danger, the man behind him had quickly struck him on the back of the head. Lights danced before David's eyes and blackness engulfed him. But, before he could fall, the man who had delivered the blow had grabbed him from the rear as the side door of the van opened. Another man jumped out to help lift David's limp body into the van. The kidnapping had taken only a few seconds as the van turned a corner and sped away.

The men inside the van covered David's head with a pillow case and tied it at the neck. They did not speak at all so they could protect their identities.

In thirty minutes' duration, they had delivered David to the address agreed upon with Youngblood. They deposited David's body in an easy chair. They tied up both his hands and ankles, and then tied them together to completely immobilize him. When they were satisfied that his escape would be impossible, they left, locking the door behind them.

David came to shortly after they left. His head hurt, but he could not rub it. When he opened his eyes and saw cloth, he felt both panic and fear.

"My ankles and hands are tied! I can't even move! Why? What on Earth is going on here?" he thought, thoroughly alarmed now.

Try as he might, David came up with more questions than answers.

While he tried to figure out his quandary, the men who had kidnapped him stopped at a corner public pay phone to call Youngblood about the delivery. They also verified that their money was at its prearranged location. Then they simply sped away into the night.

CHAPTER 22

Time seemed to stand still for David. It seemed like an eternity had passed when, actually, only a few hours had elapsed. He heard the door lock turn and a door opened. It was followed by the sound of footsteps approaching him.

A voice spoke in a deep conversational tone, "Well, here you are, David Michaels. Hopefully, you are none the worse for wear."

"Who are you and why have you kidnapped me?" asked David.

Curtis Youngblood responded, "Let's just say I'm one who is very interested in your particular talents. I just figured that kidnapping you would be the only way I could get your undivided attention on a little problem I have."

"What kind of problem?" asked David, still fearful but also curious.

"OK, here's my proposal," returned Curtis. "My son, Nathan, has a health problem. I've taken him to many doctors over the years. They can't seem to find anything wrong with him, but he's listless and without any real energy. He doesn't play like other boys, and he has no real appetite. He picks at his food, and doesn't eat enough to keep a bird alive. You heal him, and I'll set you free. It's as simple as that!"

David knew instinctively that he must exercise extreme caution in his denial, but at the same time, he needed to get as much information as possible.

"I don't know what you're talking about," David replied. "Who told you such a wild tale anyway?"

"Don't play with me!" the man spat. "Besides, I had a little chat with Doctor Hollis. You remember him, don't you?"

David's heart sank momentarily, but he summoned his courage and bravely replied, "Doctor Hollis quizzed me about some mysterious healing power, too, but I didn't know what he was talking about either."

David could hear the man as he sneered at that.

"I am not about to be put off so easily, David. Your rebuttal sounds pretty weak to me. You might as well come clean, and do what I've asked you to do. Otherwise, you'll be here for a long, long time," he retorted.

"I honestly don't know what you're talking about. If I'm going to be here for a long time, would you at least untie my hands from my ankles? My hands and ankles will still be tied, and I can't go anywhere bound up like this," said David.

"Sure, there's no reason you can't be more comfortable," spoke the man as he moved over and worked on the hard-tied knots.

To himself, he thought, "Maybe this small gesture will cause David to reconsider helping me with Nate."

When he had finished, he checked the remaining knots. Satisfied, he moved over and sat on the sofa.

David was able to lean back now in the easy chair. Now he was able to raise his tied hands above his head. He knew this could later prove useful to him.

"Well, how about it?" asked Curtis softly.

"I'd really like to help you, but I don't understand how you think I can help your son," replied David.

At the end of his patience, Curtis Youngblood let out his breath in an explosive blast.

"OK, I guess we'll have to do this the hard way!" he told David.

He moved quickly over to David, grabbed his shirt front, lifted him bodily up from the chair, and then punched him hard in the stomach.

The air exploded out David's mouth in a loud, "Whoosh!"

Now Curtis' voice became low and threatening, saying, "How about it, you little punk?"

Then he started slapping David's head hard from side to side.

Lights danced and swam before David's eyes. He felt dizzy and weak.

Again he said, "I'd like to help you, but I just can't! You have made a mistake!"

"All right," snarled the man. "We'll play your little game, but I can guarantee you that I'll win. I always win! You'll get both hungry and thirsty! I'm in no hurry. Besides,

I'll enjoy slapping you around until you see things my way!"

Curtis Youngblood turned towards the door and unlocked it.

He spoke before leaving, "This will go on day after day, and I won't be either hungry or thirsty. But you will be both! You'd better think about that and reconsider changing both your attitude and your answer before I come back!"

When David made no reply, he closed the door forcefully, locking it behind him.

David knew this man could eventually force him to give in, using hunger and thirst to break him down. His stomach still hurt, and his head was still ringing. He strained his ears for a long while, listening for any telltale signs that his captor might be silently watching him.

When he was satisfied that he was indeed alone, he raised his hands to rub his head to remove the pain from both the slaps and the back of his head. He had no idea what he had been struck with by his abductors. Instantly, the pain subsided. Next, he removed the pain from his stomach area.

"How can I set myself free?" he thought. "I need to get out of this mess!"

He tried to untie the hard knot in the cord securing the pillow case around his neck. It was awkward going, at best.

Suddenly, a bright light appeared before his covered eyes, and a pleasant female voice said, "David?"

"Miranda!" exclaimed David, happily.

Quickly, the pillow case was lifted from his head. Miranda stood before him as radiant as ever. She was smiling at him.

"David, why are you tied up?" she asked in mock disbelief.

Of course, she had been monitoring him closely, but she had been unable to intercede with the situation until now. He Who Summons would not give her permission to do so until that moment, as the course of human choices could not be interrupted yet.

Briefly, David explained what had occurred. He nodded towards his bound hands and feet.

Miranda quickly moved her hands over the ropes on his wrists, and the ropes fell to the floor.

"David, you have the power to do this for yourself! Think about it for a moment. If you can fuse atoms, molecules and matter, why can't you simply separate them?" she asked.

Recognition of this information brought a big smile to his face.

Miranda grinned and said, "Do you want to try removing the ropes on your ankles?"

Without hesitation, David concentrated on moving his hands over the ropes, which immediately fell to the floor in a pile.

"David, there are no ropes, chains, bars, locked rooms, or anything else that can hold you against your will," she spoke softly.

"Miranda, I just never thought about it before, but obviously you're right!" David replied. "The man who kidnapped me wanted to force me to use my power to cure his son for him."

"I know," replied Miranda. "His name is Curtis Youngblood. He is not only rich, but also powerful with many contacts. I don't believe that he's really a bad man—he's just misguided! He must really love his son, Nathan, to go to such extreme lengths to have him healed."

Miranda took David's hands in hers and said, "David, I want you to listen to me. Your Mother has Lung Cancer. She needs you very much right now."

"Wow! There just seems to be no end to problems!" he gasped.

She squeezed his hands while speaking, "At least, this is one problem you can solve very quickly. Why don't you head home and take care of your Mom?"

David gave Miranda a weak smile, saying, "It'll be a long walk home because I don't have any money for bus fare."

She laughed and said, "I'll bet you've forgotten. Why don't you check your pockets anyway?"

David shoved his hand into his jeans' pocket and fished out a neatly folded ten dollar bill. He gave Miranda a puzzled look.

Miranda chuckled and said, "I told you that you had probably forgotten. Now get out of here! Go get a taxi and take care of your Mom!"

"Gee, thanks a lot, Miranda!" he said as he turned and walked out the front door, which had opened before him—no longer locked, of course.

CHAPTER 23

David paid the taxi driver and went up on the porch to enter the front door, but before he could put his key into the lock, the door was opened by his mother. She stepped aside to let him in. He could see she had been crying.

She asked in a rush of concern, "Where have you been? I've been worried sick about you!"

"I'm OK, Mom. Really, I am," David said to reassure her.

"Just look at you, young man. You look terrible! Your clothes are all messed up! You are such a neat boy. It's after dark! You didn't answer me—where have you been?"

David thought, "This would be a wonderful opportunity to begin healing my Mom by giving her a big hug to calm her down. I will be able to move my hands up and down over her back to begin the healing process. If I do it just right, I'll be able to heal her without arousing her suspicion. After all, she's a very good nurse."

With this in mind, he hugged her and moved his hands, using his special power as he planned to do.

As he did so, he spoke into her ear, "I was kidnapped, Mom, by a man, and I believe he must have mistaken me for someone else. That's why I look like I do."

Startled, Julie immediately pulled free from his embrace and took a good look at him. She could see the dirt smudges on his clothes from the incident.

"Son, I think we should call the Aurora Police and report this incident! He may try to catch you again, mistake or not! How did you even get away?" she asked.

"Mom, I'm all right now. I'm home. I'm OK. I don't want to call the Police for the simple reason that I don't need the added distraction because I have school work to catch up, and I want to graduate with my class. It's only a few weeks away. Besides, I'm not hurt, see?" as he turned around so she could get a good look at him.

David pulled her into his arms again and continued to hug her in his new special way.

"David, what's with all this hugging?" she asked.

"I'm trying to make up for lost time!" he said, laughing.

She joined him, laughing as well.

David knew his Mom was enjoying the attention, as well as his hugs.

He thought, "I just can't tell her that I will deal with Curtis Youngblood in my own way and in my own time!" he promised himself silently.

CHAPTER 24

The next morning, Curtis Youngblood went to unlock the door to the room where he had left David tied up on the chair. To his shock and surprise, the door was not only unlocked, but the boy was gone!

"I know I locked that door last night before I left! How could he have escaped?" he said excitedly.

He bent over to pick up the ropes used to secure David.

"These ropes look like they've been cut with a red hot knife—the ends look fused! What is going on here anyway?" he said aloud.

He was getting more confused by the minute. Anger bubbled up to the surface at this turn of events.

"This is not how I planned for this to go!" he exclaimed.

He sat down on the sofa to think about the situation, now changed drastically from his original plans.

"What if the boy reported his kidnapping to the Police?" he thought.

This line of thought did not make him very happy. He was worried as he drove his car to work.

As he sat down at his desk, he thought, "As a last resort, I can deny that the incident ever took place. David can prove nothing because there's no evidence it ever occurred! With all the important contacts I have, it will be my word against the word of a young punk! No one would believe him. After all, I am a very important man in this town!"

With that thought, he smiled confidently.

"I'll just take those ropes and throw them into a garbage dumpster, and no one will ever be the wiser!"

He opened his drawer to pull out a cigar, lit it, and then leaned back in his chair.

"Yes, sir, next time, it will turn out a whole lot differently! I'll see to that!" he stated adamantly.

CHAPTER 25

David realized that Youngblood would never let the matter drop, so he had made a simple plan and began its execution.

The next day, he got Curtis Youngblood's address from the phone directory and located the nearest elementary school to that address. He made a couple of phone calls to the Registrar's Office, which verified that Nathan was enrolled there. With a few more questions, David learned when classes started and school let out for the day. He hung around across from the school. He just casually asked boys in the area for Nathan and was able to identify him easily. Then he left the area.

On the following day, David lounged around by a drug store. When Nathan came by, David approached him from the rear and touched the boy on the back of his head, which caused him to experience a dizzy spell. David dropped his arm over the boy's shoulder and guided him into an alley. Very quickly, he ran his hands a couple of inches from the boy's body, probing for abnormalities or blockages.

"Why, there's nothing wrong with Nathan!" he thought. "This does not surprise me at all. In fact, the problem is that he does not measure up to his father's expectations, which is something that can't be cured!"

David walked the boy back out to the sidewalk with his arm still over his shoulder. As they reached the sidewalk, David again touched the boy's head and the dizziness disappeared as fast as it had come.

Nathan looked at David in a confused way and spoke, "What just happened to me?"

David responded, "You looked like you were going to faint, and I happened to be behind you. I saw you wobbling as you walked, so I just grabbed you and helped you so you would not fall. Are you all right now?"

"Yeah, I think so," replied Nathan.

"Do you live very far from here?" asked David.

"Nah, I'm only a couple of blocks from home," Nathan answered. "Thanks for your help anyway. That's really weird, because I've never been that dizzy before now. I felt like I was going to pass out."

David smiled at him and said, "I think you'll be OK now. You probably just need to eat something."

"Yeah, maybe so," Nathan said as he walked away.

"Now," David thought, "one down and one to go! This time, my meeting with Curtis Youngblood will most definitely not go like he originally planned!"

CHAPTER 26

David made several phone calls that night, locating Curtis Youngblood's office.

"Tomorrow, I'll just pay him a little visit. I think that, by the time I am finished with him, he'll be more than glad to leave me alone—for the rest of my life!" he promised himself.

Early the next morning, David went to the car dealership where Curtis Youngblood had his office and let himself in by simply tripping the locks on the doors. Once inside, he went to the man's office. He hid inside the office coat closet, which was behind the desk, and waited patiently.

After a while, he heard Youngblood's loud voice saying, "Good morning! Please see to it that I am not disturbed! I have something I need to do."

The office door opened and closed. In a few minutes, he heard him on the phone.

"No, you bumbling idiot! He got away three days ago! I am going to need your services again, but I'll need more than you did last time."

David let himself into the office and moved up quietly behind the man. Quickly, he reached and moved his hands over Youngblood's hand that held the phone. The hand disappeared as the phone fell clattering to the desk.

"What the devil?" he muttered when he saw the phone lying on the desk.

Then he moved his arm to pick up the phone again and saw that his hand was gone.

Curtis then made a croaking sound of disbelief, and his face mirrored his surprise and shock.

David moved quickly around to the front of the desk, picked up the phone and set it back in its cradle.

"Hello, Mr. Youngblood. Do you remember me? No, I suppose not. The last time we were together, my head was covered by a pillow case, wasn't it?" said David matter-of-factly. "Can I suppose that you were planning a second kidnapping for me, then? That is what it sounded like to me."

Curtis was groaning out loud by then. He stopped it for a moment and said abrasively, "What did you do to my hand, Michaels?"

David responded, "I just want you to know what I can and will do to you if you ever provoke me again. I could have made you disappear altogether just as easily! Now I want you to listen to me very closely. I've examined Nathan, and he is completely normal. Because he doesn't meet your expectations is not his fault. Nathan's interests and desires just lay in other directions. Now, when I leave this office, our business is finished—permanently! You are not to mention me or what just happened to anyone—not ever! If you swear to uphold this agreement, I'll restore your hand. So, what's it going to be?"

David had intentionally used a language which he knew Curtis Youngblood would understand—power.

The man looked at David for a few moments and then said, "I thought you just used your power to heal people."

David smiled slowly at him and said, "I do, but you have forced me to change my tactics. So, what's it going to be? I have other business to tend to, and I need to leave."

David began turning towards the door.

Curtis exhaled resignedly and humbly said, "I want my hand back, please."

David turned towards him, looked him straight in the eye and held his gaze.

"Do you swear to me that you will uphold the agreement I've just outlined?" he asked.

"Yes, yes, I do," he stammered, with fear in his voice.

"OK," replied David, "but I also believe you owe me a sincere apology for roughing me up."

Curtis lowered his eyes and spoke softly, "I'm very sorry that I mistreated you. I won't do it ever again, to anybody!"

David felt that the apology was sincere and that he would, indeed, keep his word about the agreement. He moved his hands over the man's stump of an arm. As the hand began to materialize, a moan escaped Curtis Youngblood's lips. It was a sound of joy and amazement. When the hand had been fully restored, David looked into the eyes of a very changed man.

He spoke firmly to him: "You know, if I were you, I think I would just try to be a good Dad to Nathan and set a good example for him. Don't try to make him into something he isn't. Talk with him. Listen to him. Spend time with him. Do things with him that he likes to do. You might be surprised at the results!"

With that said and his business completed, David turned and left the office.

He thought to himself as he was leaving, "It's very unlikely I'll have any more trouble from him!"

Whistling as he walked away, he felt a burden lift off his shoulders.

On Gorbandihar, Miranda looked at He Who Summons with a smile and said, "You were right again. David did resolve the matter peacefully."

He Who Summons just returned her smile, saying, "Yes, he did at that."

CHAPTER 27

During the next several days, David could tell by the feedback through his hands, as well as the healthy change in his Mom's complexion, that her healing was indeed taking place.

"Man, once the healing is complete, Mom will be forced to endure a lot of questions from her doctors, which might cause her a dilemma. However, since she knows nothing, there's nothing she can tell them," David thought, smiling. "I am safe. Dr. Hollis will not be alone when it comes to medical bafflement!"

Just as he had figured, his Mom had been questioned repeatedly when her x-rays revealed that she was indeed Cancer-free.

David thought, "I cannot remember seeing Mom so happy! It's a wonderful feeling to be able to cure her!"

Thinking about it brought a lump to his throat.

"She thinks the healing is just from the power of prayer," he said to himself, chuckling. "In a way, though, that really is true. After all, He Who Summons had this in

147

mind from the very beginning of my training. I can now heal others. Just think of the hullabaloo it will cause! Well, I'm sure it will die down after a while."

It did, in fact, happen as David had anticipated.

The time flew by for David. He had taken his sweetheart, Melody, to the prom, and it had been a wonderful occasion for them. It was shortly after the prom that he and Melody became engaged. After he graduated from high school, he realized his life was really only beginning. He was anxious to see what would come around the corner next. Like most young people, he was eager to move forward with his life. At times, he became frustrated and impatient because events did not keep pace with his desires.

CHAPTER 28

Time passed, and David was getting ready for bed one night.

He thought, "Time seems to be simply flying so fast. I think back to the period of time I spent curing my Mom and, of course, taking my sweetheart to my high school prom. It was like it just happened yesterday, when in actuality it occurred over a year and a half ago!"

"I have two goals to work towards, both of which occupy most of my thoughts and energy. Even with the vast amount of knowledge I now possess since my trip to Gorbandihar, I can't tell anyone about it. Without a degree, I won't be able to marry my sweetheart, Melody Ann, or support her as my wife."

Like many young people, he struggled to control his impatience.

He had succeeded in finding employment as a floor salesman at a local furniture store and worked very hard to earn commissions.

He continued contemplating his current circumstances and thought, "But it seems like, regardless of how much effort I exert, I just cannot seem to make any headway towards achieving my goals. Melody and I have discussed marriage so many times over the past one and one-half years, especially during the long walks we take on my days off. She's agreeable to the marriage and obviously loves me very much. We are growing closer and closer in our relationship, but I know in my heart that I cannot take care of her on my meager salary as a salesman. I know my Mom approves of our marriage, so the only fly in the ointment is a lack of money! I want to marry Melody as soon as I can and even start a family, but in my present circumstances, I just cannot see a way to do it!"

He put on his pajamas and lay on his bed.

"In fact, I'm undecided about whether to tell Melody we will have to put our marriage on hold until either I complete college or make more money somehow!"

Reaching over with a sigh of resignation, he turned out the bedroom lamp.

CHAPTER 29

David was at work, closing a deal on a sofa set with an affluent lady.

As he did the paperwork, he was thinking, "I can't help but notice her gold jewelry. She must be very rich because she's wearing a gold watch, a gold necklace, gold ear rings, and a heavy gold bracelet. They are very expensive-looking! They must have cost a fortune!"

After she left the store, David was still thinking about her gold.

"I sure wish I had some gold!"

As he continued to think about it, he thought, "Why can't I make some gold? Miranda said I couldn't accept money or pay for any healing I did, but she didn't say I couldn't make some gold!"

David was beside himself with excitement.

"Alchemy! Why didn't I think of this before now? If I am successful, then I can marry Melody! We wouldn't have to wait at all!" he thought. "I can't just quit my job because, if my efforts are unsuccessful, I will still need a steady income to pay for my college."

Very quietly, he began gathering all the materials together that he would need to accomplish his task of making gold. He decided he would work on the weekends in the basement of the small house in the area of Fitzsimons Army Medical Center, which he and his Mom had been renting since he had graduated from high school.

The rest of the day and the next four days seemed to drag forever until Friday evening finally arrived.

When he began focusing on the transformation, he was totally amazed at how easy it was to make the gold. He decided to make placer gold as it was the easiest to convert to cash, and it would not draw undue attention to him.

"I can always say I got it gold panning. After all, they did find gold in the local creeks back in the 1800's," he thought, "and they still do."

"Wow! Gold! Imagine that! Can you believe it?" he said out loud excitedly.

He smiled to himself, musing, "I can be as rich as I choose. I can afford anything my mind can conceive or dream about! Too bad I didn't think of this sooner!"

In fact, he was so busy thinking about what he could buy with the gold that he just completely forgot that his thoughts and deeds were being monitored and recorded on Gorbandihar. Helping or healing someone was the farthest thing from his mind. All he could think about was making enough gold to take care of his own personal desires.

CHAPTER 30

Miranda hurried towards the Receiving Room of He Who Summons and stopped inside a dome-covered archway at its entrance.

She was already prepared to wait for an acknowledgement so she could enter when a deep, mellow voice said, "Come in, Miranda."

When she entered, He was standing with His hands resting on the window sill and was peering out the huge glass window.

As she approached, He spoke without turning towards her, "I take it that your visit has something to do with our young Earthling, David?"

"Yes, good Master, it does," she responded.

Turning now to face her, there was a small smile on His face. His hair was white and shoulder length, and His eyes were a sparkling blue. Standing at six feet in height, He wore a floor-length, blue satin robe.

Miranda smiled back automatically, partly because His smile always affected her— as if He knew something no one else knew.

"Well, what is it all about, Miranda?" He asked.

"Good Master," she responded, "I've received patterns from David Michaels' thought processes that are somewhat disturbing."

She proceeded to explain the complete situation and finished by saying, "Now he is making gold!"

"But, Miranda," He said, "didn't you explain that he was not to use the knowledge for personal enrichment?"

"Good Master," she said, "I instructed him that he was not to receive any pay or reward for his healing or services, but nothing was said about him making silver or gold. I thought I had followed Your instructions to the best of my understanding."

"You're absolutely right, Miranda. As I recall the instructions didn't cover his ability to make gold, using his new-found knowledge," He said. "The lad is very creative and inventive, but I think he violates the very spirit of what We taught him and why. I just didn't think We needed to cover every small detail."

Miranda listened and considered a moment before she spoke, saying, "Good Master, We could bring him back here for more explanation, or, as a last resort, You could simply revoke his powers. The second option will result in no more blunders or mistakes on his part and therefore no more worrisome behaviors."

He responded, "Miranda, the latter option would erase the good We sought to bring about by bringing him here to teach him in the first place. No, I don't believe that will be necessary. You see, Miranda, when he focuses on only the material world around him and does not use his powers for good, as We designed it, the more they will diminish. That would not be good for David or for Our plans. I was so hoping that he would choose to do well, and maybe in the future, We could train others or even train him to train others of his kind. We know from long study that Earthlings are basically good—and, with help, they can achieve great accomplishments."

She said, "Oh, yes, I agree completely with what You say. Maybe We could just do nothing for awhile and observe his future choices and actions. If he proceeds with deeds strictly for personal gain, We'll know, and if he decides to use his powers as We intended, We will also know. The proof will be in the way his future unfolds, for good or ill, and whether his powers expand or diminish, yes?"

He responded, "The lad shows great promise, Miranda, and I want very much for him to succeed. Because I trust your logic and clear thinking, We will wait and observe Our young man in all his future endeavors—very closely, Miranda, very closely indeed!"

"As you wish, Good Master," she said with a small curtsy.

Miranda then turned and departed the Receiving Room.

CHAPTER 31

Miranda set about monitoring David's thoughts and deeds on a regular basis. She had other duties and responsibilities to be sure, but she also had explicit instructions from He Who Summons.

Time passed and the monitoring continued. Miranda made note that two years (as the Earthlings kept time) had passed. Many things had taken place, and she had kept a concise record. She had kept the Good Master updated on a regular basis, as instructed.

Looking over her records, she thought, "To date, David has bought and paid for a home, a new automobile and clothing. Of course, he married Melody and paid for an expensive wedding ceremony and honeymoon. He's placed a sizeable amount into a savings account as well. Oh, yes, another important event has occurred in David and Melody's life—she gave birth to a fine baby boy whom they named Jonathan, and he is now one year old. Just looking at all of this, I can see that these last two years, David has not concerned himself with anything outside his little family. He's not healed anyone or done anything with his powers as We first proposed. I guess the time has now come to talk to He Who Summons, as He instructed me."

A deep sigh escaped her lips at the thought. She made a couple more notations on her pad, placed it in a folder, and left for the Master's Receiving Room.

As she was on the way, she thought, "I personally do not want to see David having problems with his powers. After all, I did teach him and have watched him grow in knowledge and ability. If only he would have chosen to use it as We intended!"

CHAPTER 32

David and Melody were very happy in their new home. Life was very good for them. In addition, there was an abundance of everything that was needed: Food, clothing, a car, and money.

David had become totally immersed in his desire to provide for his little family. In his concentrated effort, he found little time for anything else.

His plan was to make at least one more batch of gold and then stop for awhile so he could devote all his time to his wife and son.

He was in the basement working when Melody called down to him. Her voice was filled with concern.

"David! Come up here quickly!"

He had never heard Melody use that tone of voice before, and it startled him.

"Coming," he hollered up the stairs as he got up.

He was thinking, "That is so strange! For some reason, I am not having any luck making the transformation from base metal to gold anyway. I'm stumped! I'm really at a dead end. This has never happened before. I know, I've had increasing difficulty over time, but this is ridiculous!"

When he got upstairs, Melody was obviously very near a panic, with tears in her eyes.

She said, "Jonathan is running a high temperature, and we'll have to take him to the hospital as soon as we can!"

"Take it easy, Sweetheart. Let me see him," he responded.

Taking Jonathan in his arms, David used his hands quickly, trying to discover what the problem was.

He thought, "What's happening? I don't understand! I can't gain any information through my hands!"

Now he really began to worry.

"This has never happened since I received my powers!" he thought.

He had completely forgotten how long it had been since he had done any healing at all.

David felt panic now, but he knew he had to maintain control of his emotions. He grabbed the phone and dialed his Mom's number.

It seemed like an eternity passed before she answered, "Hello."

"Mom, it's David. We've got a problem! Jonathan is burning up with a high temperature, and he's having trouble breathing! What can we do?"

"Listen carefully, David, start sponging Jonathan down with a cool wash cloth—put him in his little tub. I'll be there in ten to fifteen minutes, I promise!" she responded.

David hung up the phone and told Melody what his Mom had told him to do for their son. They brought out his little tub, took off his clothes, and started sponging him off.

A few minutes later, Julie came into the house without bothering to knock. She went straight to the kitchen where she knew they would be. She could see they were following her instructions.

Quickly she hugged David and Melody.

"Let me see my Grandson," she said, as she began checking his pulse and taking his temperature. Then she used her stethoscope and listened to his lungs. After a minute or two, she looked into their worried faces.

She said, "I believe Jonathan probably has Pneumonia. We need to take him to the hospital Emergency Room where a doctor can do an x-ray of his chest. Melody, get a bag together with all you'll need. The sooner we can get him there, the better!"

Melody hurriedly gathered whatever she thought they might need, and they left for the hospital.

CHAPTER 33

Miranda was once again in the Master's complex, sitting in a comfortable chair waiting, with her folder on a table beside her.

She felt a certain amount of sympathy and sadness for David's plight concerning his and Melody's son. It was purely coincidence that Jonathan came down very sick shortly after David's power had completely diminished.

She heard a noise, and she automatically glanced toward the door as He Who Summons walked in.

"I'm sorry, Miranda. I hope you've not been kept waiting too long," He said, laughing. "It seems there's never enough time and too many demanding details."

His laughter was infectious.

In response, she laughed and said, "Only a few minutes, but it's always good to stop, even if it's only for a short period."

"Did you have any problems when you were keeping a watch on David?" He asked.

"None at all," she responded. "I'm just a little saddened that David and Melody's son, Jonathan, got very sick shortly after he discovered his power was apparently not there anymore."

The Master scratched His head and said, "Yes, that was a sad state of events, but it can't be helped at the moment. What I'd like you to do is take a little trip to Earth. When you get the chance to talk with David, please explain to him what the consequences are of his actions—that his focus on the material world alone is responsible for what has happened to his power. It has always been true that the focus must be placed on the unseen realm of Spirit, faith, belief, and trust as he uses his powers for good deeds. I believe that this information, coming from you personally, will help him immeasurably. I still have big hopes for that lad, you know."

"Yes, Master, I'll do my best," she said.

Miranda arose and picked up her folder and moved towards the door.

"I'll see you when I get back," she said.

"Have a good trip!" He replied as He watched her disappear through the door to Earth.

CHAPTER 34

They were at the University of Colorado Hospital. The child had been examined, x-rayed, and then diagnosed with Pneumonia, as Julie had suspected. All they could do now was wait, hope and pray.

"If I only had the power I used to have, Jonathan would have already been healed!" thought David bitterly. "How did I lose it anyway? After all, I haven't done something I wasn't supposed to do—not in my book anyway!"

David and Melody sat together, holding hands as they looked at the bed. They could not see their son very well because an oxygen tent obscured his little head and upper body.

Melody whispered, "He's so small and pale-looking, David. I'm so afraid for him! He's so little and young!"

Tears welled up in her eyes and rolled down her cheeks.

David put his arm around her shoulders and whispered in return, "Don't cry, Sweetheart! I believe Jonathan is going to be all right."

He looked at Melody and continued gently, "You wait here and I'll walk down to the Cafeteria to get us coffee and a sandwich, or would you like hot chocolate instead of coffee?"

"Hot chocolate and a sandwich would be very nice," she responded. "I'll just freshen up a bit while you are gone."

David rose and kissed her on the cheek. David smiled at her from the doorway, hoping to ease her apprehension.

"I'll be back in a few minutes," he said.

Before he left, he looked at his Mom, who was sound asleep in another chair, her head hanging forward and down.

No one knew that, while Melody was in the bathroom, Julie was sleeping, and David went to the Cafeteria, a lovely blonde lady entered Jonathan's room through a wall. She placed her hands over the boy's chest, clearing the Pneumonia from his lungs, and then hovered them over his body, removing the fever. As quickly as she had come, she was gone.

Once the Cafeteria was located and his purchases completed, David was walking back down the hallway, carrying a bag with sandwiches and balancing a tray containing the coffee and hot chocolate.

Suddenly, a door to his right side opened. Miranda stood there, beckoning him to come inside the room. David was rather startled as he entered the room.

Miranda sat down on the bed and motioned him to a chair. Carefully, he set the tray on a side table, along with his bag of sandwiches, and sat down.

"Are you surprised to see me?" asked Miranda with a smile.

"Yes, I am," replied David, "but I'm glad to see you too! I'm very upset about losing the power you taught me! What's happened to me? I need to know!"

"That's why I'm here," replied Miranda. "I know our instructions did not cover you utilizing your power to create gold on Earth. However, you were instructed to not take pay or any reward for using your power to heal anyone who needed your special gifts. Well, you used your powers solely to create gold and enrich yourself. You've purchased a house, car, furniture, and paid off bills—all in the material realm. This in and of itself is not a bad thing, but you've used all your time and efforts to create wealth! You have not accomplished any good deeds or healings! These are selfish acts because you have not had any concern for anyone else. There are severe consequences for that. Now you know what they are because your powers became less potent each time. You've lost your connection to the unseen world of Spirit, faith, belief, and trust! He Who Summons has sent me here to explain to you why your powers receded. The Master is very disappointed as He had such great hopes for you!"

David's eyes filled with tears of shame, looked at Miranda, and took a deep breath.

"I just wanted to be able to marry Melody and take good care of her—give her a home, you know? Then along came Jonathan, and we were both so very happy. I now realize that I probably misused my power, but I wasn't doing it just for myself. Now our son has come down with a high fever, and they say it's Pneumonia! He's fighting for his life! I'd give back everything I've spent the gold on if I had just enough power to heal Jonathan, but I can't feel anything! Please increase my power so I can heal him, and I'll not only stop making gold, but I'll sell everything and give it to the poor!"

Miranda was deeply touched by David's remorse.

She said, "David, that is not within my power to do. Your actions diminished your power, so you are going to have to change your focus and change your actions. Selling what you've got is not the answer. You know that your thought patterns, which generate actions, are the right answer for you. Only time will tell, David—time and your choices. I have to go now, but these need warming before I leave."

She moved her hands over the coffee and chocolate, reheating the liquid.

"I think you should know that Jonathan will be all right. I have seen to that a few moments ago. Good bye, David," she said.

Before David could speak again, Miranda had disappeared by moving through a wall in the room.

David sighed and picked up the bag of sandwiches and the tray. He left the room and carefully walked back to his son's room. Melody was still in the bathroom and his Mom was still asleep. Quietly, he placed the bag and tray on a table and moved over to the bedside to check on his son.

He thought, "It is exactly as Miranda said! Jonathan is breathing normally. He's not struggling for breath anymore—he's actually sleeping peacefully!"

Melody eased up beside David and took his hand while looking down at their son, laying her head on his shoulder.

"Do you think he's going to be OK?" she said.

David smiled down at her and said, "Yes, Melody, I know he's going to be OK!"

CHAPTER 35

The little family returned home. Jonathan had indeed recovered and was once again a happy, healthy little boy.

Two weeks had gone by, and David was now a changed man. Without any hesitation, he had cleared out all the materials for making the placer gold.

Looking at the now-empty basement, he thought, "That period of my life is finished. I've got some work to do—on me!"

David soon found a job at a car dealership, selling new and used cars. He also started to take college night classes, which kept him very busy. Between work, classes, and study, David found his time filled and challenging.

Time seemed to literally fly as he devoted himself to his family and accomplishing his dreams—only in a far different way. He was, instead, working intensely on his thought patterns. He now knew what really mattered and the consequences of his poor focus.

On a Saturday, David was doing a small chore for Melody. He was standing on a ladder, hanging a rather large picture on the wall. Once he had located the exact spot for the hanger, he drew back his hammer to strike the hanger nail. Instead, he struck his thumb with the hammer, using great force. Blood spurted out between the side of his thumb and thumbnail.

"Yikes!" he shouted as he stuck his left thumb into his mouth and immediately tasted blood.

Then he grabbed his left thumb with his right hand, and he could once more feel the heat coming forth. When he opened his right hand, he naturally expected to see a bloody mess. Instead, there was no blood and no sign of the injury!

"Wow!" he said. "Best of all, there's no pain!"

With a smile of joy on his face, David climbed down off the ladder and began dancing joyfully around the house, chanting, "Yes! Yes! Yes!"

CHAPTER 36

On Gorbandihar, He Who Summons and Miranda were watching a large color screen which had been set up to monitor David.

"Did you see how he just healed his thumb, Miranda? Since he quit solely advancing his own personal agenda, his focus on healing is naturally returning. Maybe now he'll use that power as We proposed!" He said, beaming at her.

Rising from her chair, she smiled at Him and said, "You're right, Master!" as she motioned towards her glass with her hand.

The glass rose gently from the table and began slowly moving towards her. The glass contained a cool, refreshing minty liquid—much like tea on Earth—and was consumed by all the inhabitants on Gorbandihar.

"That's a wonderful idea!" He said, as He held out His own hand to retrieve His glass. He continued, "I believe that David will be all right now that he's regained his proper focus and is beginning to direct it towards its designed purpose!"

He continued, "As you probably already know, I've been observing the Earthlings for a very long time. They are a very peculiar species. Sometimes, I look on in horror at some of the strange things they do to one another, such as war, which not only causes widespread death but such sadness, hunger and destruction. Such a waste! Then, they will show some advances in medical treatments, science and humanities to prolong life because they hold it precious. They can be stubborn, artistic, creative, and at times kind to one another. When provoked, they will unite against whatever they perceive as a wrong perpetrated against them. When I begin to wonder if they'll advance or stagnate, out they come with a new invention or breakthrough in technology. They can be very persuasive, agreeable or competitive, as witnessed by their sporting events. They possess such drive, desire, and creative ability. I'm convinced that, one day, they will be able to freely travel in space. That is why I gave David this power so he could help them along. He is My small beacon of hope there on Earth."

Miranda smiled because He Who Summons had never before spoken to her of His thoughts or reasoning so eloquently.

She said, "I have developed some of the same thoughts about the Earthlings after observing them for so long. I have enjoyed my time spent with David during his instruction. I must confess that I've been pulling for him to succeed."

He Who Summons smiled as He finished His drink and rose.

He said, "I think David will be fine, and I wanted to share My reasoning with you. I've got to go about My work now—so many details to take care of, you know, and they won't get completed on their own."

Miranda smiled and moved towards the entrance to leave, thinking, "He Who Summons rarely confides like this to anyone, and I feel honored."

CHAPTER 37

David was being discreet and was quietly going about healing people with all manner of diseases and ailments. He very secretly gave sight to the blind and hearing to the deaf. He mended broken bones, and even went about healing animals and birds where and when he got the opportunity.

The newspapers were loaded with stories about miraculous cures and impossible healings. Radio announcers and even television news reporters were constantly telling, enlarging, embellishing, and extolling the miracles—including the national news media broadcasts. Even with all the exposure, no one could identify the source, except that it was centered in the Denver Metropolitan Area in Colorado.

Best of all, David went about his chosen duties, mostly during the night time, away from prying eyes and ears. He had become very proficient at stealth and evasion in order to avoid arousing suspicion or draw attention to himself. David took great enjoyment and pride in healing, always avoiding attention or reward. This was, in essence, what Miranda and He Who Summons had wanted him to accomplish in the first place.

David had worked all day at the car dealership and had completed one of his nightly outings. He was tired after a very busy day and night. As he finished brushing his teeth and changed into his pajamas, David was already drowsy. Quietly, he slipped under the covers and gave Melody a quick kiss on the cheek. He was almost asleep as soon as his head touched the pillow.

His last thought was, "I hope He Who Summons and Miranda are happy with me now!"

CHAPTER 38

Life was very good for David and his little family. His powers now were strong. In fact, they became stronger each time he performed a healing.

David was sitting, reading the paper. He noticed an article with a picture of two people he recognized—Doctor Daniel Hollis and Nurse Betty Lewis.

"Good for them!" he thought as he whistled a little tune. "This article says they got married about three years ago. That has to be a terrific match!"

He finished his breakfast and went to work.

"How the time seems to fly by!" he thought as he walked about the dealership lot, checking inventory to see what had been sold and what cars remained. "Just think—in two more weeks, Jonathan will be five years' old already!"

At home, Jonathan was finishing his breakfast.

"Mom, can I go play with Petey?" he asked.

Melody looked at him, smiled at his excitement, and said, "Yes, you may, just as soon as you finish your food!"

"OK!" he said, stuffing the food into his mouth.

"Can I go now?" he said, with his mouth stuffed full like a little chipmunk.

Smiling at him, Melody said, "Yes."

He ran out the door almost as soon as she said it.

Melody thought about their next door neighbor's little boy, Petey, who was about Jonathan's age. They played together almost daily and were close buddies.

"Tom and Elsa Waverly are really wonderful neighbors. We've become good friends in this last year since they moved here," she thought.

All was going well on this fine sunny day, and the boys were hard at play. Elsa gave the boys a cold, tall glass of sweetened sun tea to help cool them down and then went back into the house.

Petey lost his grip on the glass and his balance almost simultaneously. The glass fell and broke into pieces. The base of the glass, however, contained a very large and sharp piece, which was pointing upwards. When Petey lost his balance and fell, his leg landed on the base, cutting a deep, two-inch gash just below the knee. He screamed out in pain as blood gushed out of the wound.

Jonathan, seeing all that blood, ran towards the back door calling, "Mrs. Elsa, come quickly—Petey's hurt!"

Elsa had already heard Petey's scream and was heading out the back door.

Upon seeing the amount of blood on the patio and on Petey's leg, she cried out in fear and anguish, "Oh, my!"

She bent over to check out the cut on Petey's leg. Very quickly, she ran back into the house to retrieve a clean towel. Returning, she grabbed Petey's leg and wrapped the cut leg tightly, applying pressure to stop the flow of blood.

She looked at Jonathan and told him, "Jonathan, run and get your Mother. Tell her I need her help. Run quickly now!"

Jonathan ran off to fetch his mother.

Petey was still crying loudly, and Elsa talked soothingly to him to calm him down.

Very quickly, Melody and Jonathan ran up.

Breathlessly, Melody saw the blood and blurted out, "What in the world happened?"

"He fell and cut himself on that glass. I need your help!" Elsa responded. "Let's get him into the car. You can sit with him and Jonathan in the back, and keep pressure on the cut while I drive. Can you do that for me?" asked Elsa with a pleading look on her face.

"Why, of course, I'll help. Let's get him into the car," returned Melody.

Turning to Jonathan, she said, "Run and turn off the television for Mommy, please, and come back quickly."

Jonathan took off, running as fast as his little legs would go, and returning the same way.

By the time they arrived at the Emergency Room of the University of Colorado Hospital, the cut was a mess.

Upon arrival at the Hospital, Melody had called David and explained what had happened.

"I'll be there as soon as I can," he told her.

Doctor Hollis and Nurse Betty Hollis were on duty in the Emergency Room. Their turn had come to work there. The couple was actually enjoying the duty change.

Doctor Hollis saw the bloody towel and moved Petey to a bed, while Nurse Betty pulled a privacy curtain around it. She checked to make sure the Doctor had all the necessary equipment he would need. Once the towel was removed, Doctor Hollis gently probed for glass fragments. Upon finding none, he administered a pain-deadening shot to Petey's leg. After preparing and cleaning the laceration, he began stitching the wound. He worked swiftly and professionally. He then stood back and gave the neat bandage his nod of approval.

All during Petey's treatment, Elsa was by his side. She admired the efficient skill displayed by Doctor Hollis.

"He's so good with children," she thought. "I wonder if he has any?"

In the meantime, David walked into the Emergency Room and hugged Melody. He looked at Jonathan, who had been silent. Melody told him that he had been that way since getting into the car and while waiting in the Hospital.

"Are you all right, Sport?" he asked Jonathan as he lifted his son from a chair and hugged him, too.

Tears began to flow down Jonathan's face as he sobbed out the words, "Petey's hurt, Dad! He's hurt real bad! He's losing all his blood! Will he die?"

David responded softly, "He'll be fine, Son. I know Doctor Hollis, and he won't let anything happen to him. You'll see what I mean in a few minutes."

Sure enough, the curtains opened, and Doctor Hollis, with Nurse Betty's help, lifted Petey from the bed to his feet. Petey stood still for a few seconds, and then took a tentative step. He walked towards Jonathan with a limp, but his face wore a little smile.

"Hi, Jonathan!" Petey said as he took a chair beside his friend.

"Hello, Petey!" replied Jonathan as the words just tumbled out: "Does your leg hurt a lot? Does it hurt when you walk? I was so scared. You were bleeding so bad!"

As he spoke, he held his hand over Petey's bandaged knee. He really did not know why, but he could feel heat emanating from his little hand.

After a little while, Petey jumped down from his chair, looked at Jonathan and laughed.

"Let's go home and play pitch and catch. I want to use my new glove!" Petey said.

He ran over to his mother without even a limp and asked, "Can we go home now, Mom? Jonathan and I want to play."

Doctor Hollis had been watching Petey very closely.

Acting on a hunch, he said, "Petey, I want you to come over here. I want to check the knee before you leave."

"OK," Petey said.

Doctor Hollis lifted Petey up and sat him on the edge of the bed. Quickly, he removed the bandage just as Nurse Betty walked over. She was also very curious. Elsa, David, Melody and Jonathan came over as well.

When Doctor Hollis removed the bandage, he was shocked and puzzled to find the stitches lying inside the bandage, with no evidence of the wound on the knee. Nurse Betty's mouth fell open as a gasp of surprise escaped her lips. Melody and Elsa exchanged looks of amazement. They all looked bewildered, except for David. He had watched Jonathan move his hand over Petey's bandaged knee.

Doctor Hollis turned towards David and held out the bandage with the stitches embedded in the gauze part of the wrapping. There was a questioning look on his face.

David looked at Doctor Hollis, shrugged his shoulders, and held his hands palm out. The gesture said plainly, "I don't know!"

David thought as he gathered everyone together to leave, "I cannot imagine how it happened, but genetic transfer has occurred! Jonathan has inherited my power to heal, and he's only five years' old! He's not been trained, but he possesses a loving, caring heart! What will He Who Summons and Miranda think of this?"

Later, as he was driving back to work, David began contemplating the impact of what had happened, and then he started to laugh. In fact, he laughed until his ribs hurt!

On Gorbandihar, both He Who Summons and Miranda were watching the screens and laughing, mirroring David's reaction to what had just occurred.

THE END OF BOOK ONE